Extracurricular

D.G. Whiskey

DEDICATION

To Steffi. For an unforgettable time in Saigon.

CONTENTS

ACKNOWLEDGMENTS

I'd like to extend my sincerest thanks to the readers who reach out and let me know how my writing has touched them—it humbles me greatly and is truly the reason why I write. I love to hear from you, so please don't be shy!

PART 1

1
LANDON

A pair of hands slipped over my eyes just as I lifted the glass of whiskey to my lips.

"Guess who?"

The woman's voice was low and sexy in my ear, intimate in a way that sent a shiver down the back of my neck.

There was only one problem—I didn't recognize the voice.

It wasn't too loud in the bar. The hangout spot near Harvard's campus was a favorite for undergrads and graduate students alike. It had a relaxed atmosphere where groups of friends could go to chat without having to shout over loud music.

My mind raced through names, faces, and voices of the many women I knew in the area but came up empty. Something in that sultry voice prodded my memory, but I couldn't figure out what it was.

"I would recognize that voice anywhere," I lied. "It's the voice of an angel."

When all else fails, deliver a compliment.

The hands fell away from my face and one of them slapped my shoulder. "Landy! You are too sweet."

I froze at the name. No one had called me *Landy* in years. Not since I left Boulder for Boston and never looked back.

A slender brunette with gracefully curling hair tumbling around her shoulders slipped onto the barstool next to mine with a wide smile on her face. That face was like the voice—faintly familiar, an echo of the distant past. The combination of face, voice, and her old pet name for me was enough to make the connection.

"Addy?"

The smile turned into a grin. "It's been a long time. You're looking great, Landon."

"You're one to talk! What happened to you?"

The last time I'd seen Adeline Hudson, she'd been a precocious preteen. My best friend's little sister. The annoying but adorable and awkward girl who'd always wanted to tag along with everything the older boys did.

Now she was a full-blown woman with a beautiful face and winning smile, and the way she filled out the tight black dress she wore...

I can't look at her like that. She's Addy! Nick would kill me.

Plus it just felt weird. She may as well have been my own kid sister with the amount of time I'd spent at their house growing up.

2

"I grew up," she said with a twinkle in her eye.

I flushed as I realized that she had just seen the way my eyes had trailed down her body and widened at the sight.

"Apparently! I mean, damn, Addy, you could stop a guy's heart just by looking at him."

She put her hand on my chest and frowned. "It feels like it's ticking along just fine. I need to work on my touch."

That brilliant smile flashed a moment later, and we shared a laugh. Addy took her time removing her hand, and the contact sent a surge of blood through my body. I shifted to hide the growing bulge in my jeans.

How the hell did she get so hot? She used to be such a nerdy kid.

"Nick mentioned you were coming to town for school. He said you'd probably come by our place to check it out. When did you get in?"

"Just two days ago! It's been so much fun so far. It's amazing how many friends I've made already. I came out tonight with a few people from my dorm."

I'd been ignoring my own friends, but they barely noticed. They were used to my tendency to wander off and talk to women. "Aren't you too young for a bar?"

Addy shrugged. "I'm only eighteen, but I've had a fake ID for a year now."

I fought to contain the reaction her words caused. She was only eighteen. It wasn't fair. Not with the way she tilted her head to the side and slipped her gaze along my muscular shoulders and arms. She wasn't the only one who had improved their looks since we last met.

With an inward groan, I fought to keep my eyes on her face. The eyes and nose that had been too big for her face as a child were now the perfect size, and her features had gained a mature but still youthful elegance.

It had been so long since I'd talked to her, and as we caught up, it grew harder to connect the child she'd been with the woman she'd become. There was too vast a gulf between my memories and the vivacious person in front of me.

She was intoxicating.

"I just finished my PhD in business economics and am beginning my assistant professorship to continue my research. I actually teach my first class tomorrow." I finished my recap of the past several years. It wasn't very exciting, the academic research I'd spent the past several years completing, but I was immensely proud of it. I was young to accomplish as much in my field as I had.

Instead of the glazed-eye reaction I expected, Addy leaned forward and put her hand on my thigh. "That's amazing, Landon! Congratulations, that must feel so good!"

Not as good as that hand on my thigh.

Did she know she was only a couple of inches away from my cock?

"It really does. What about you, though? What else have you

been doing besides becoming way too attractive and breaking hearts?"

Her hand squeezed my thigh and I nearly died.

"Oh, stop. I'm the same girl I always was. I just know how to do my makeup now, and I run all the time."

I shook my head. "Bullshit. You're hot and you know it."

Addy bit her lip and tilted her head to the side. "You think so?"

The look sent another flood of blood through my body, and my cock grew a little more and twitched.

She looked down at my leg and suddenly realized where her hand was—she'd felt the movement in my jeans. Pink blossomed on her cheeks as she saw the obvious bulge so close to her hand.

I held my breath as she looked back up at me with wide eyes.

ADELINE

All conscious thoughts fled my mind, save one.

I want him so badly.

It wasn't a new thought. Landon had been my first crush, the one every girl had that was so unrealistic that it could never come true. He'd been the basis of my preteen fantasies when I started to explore my body, cementing his special place in my heart and mind.

I'd known they would never come true, not when he was so much older than me.

Now, his hard cock was an inch away from my hand, his thigh hot under my palm, and I had a decision to make. My reaction would determine how the night would go, and maybe the rest of our lives.

Fighting back the instinct to recoil and apologize, I left my hand where it was.

Fortune favors the bold.

"I guess you do think I'm hot," I said. I winked and hoped it looked like the sexy, confident and flirtatious gesture I intended and not an off-putting leer. Pursuing guys wasn't my strong suit.

"Of course I do, Addy. Look at you," he said. "It's inappropriate, though. You're only eighteen, and you're Nick's little sister. I'm sorry. Let's forget it."

His mouth said one thing, but even in my short time dating in high school, I'd learned what it meant when a boy looked at me like that. The big difference was that Landon was no boy. He was a full man, and just being around him made me feel drunk and giddy. I didn't want it to stop.

"Come on, Landon. We're just talking. There's nothing wrong with that."

His eyes burned into mine. By instinct, I removed my hand from his thigh and stretched my arms behind my back, pushing my chest forward. The plunging neckline of my tight dress emphasized my assets, and the movement pushed my breasts out. Landon's gaze dropped to my chest and his jaw fell open as he stared.

I smiled, the response automatic. Teasing and tormenting men was a female right, and I loved exercising that right when it got me what I wanted. And what I wanted was Landon's mouth on mine.

The past seven years had treated him well. He'd been in decent shape in high school, but nothing compared to the broad shoulders and sharp jaw he had now. The simple gray v-neck he wore clung to his body and made it clear how muscled he'd gotten.

He fought to lift his eyes back to my face. "Addy, that's not fair."

"Who said anything about being fair?" I asked. I put my hand back on his thigh and slid it an inch higher. He flinched as my finger brushed something hard.

Landon's eyes fell closed, and the muscles in his jaw jumped. "Addy…" His hand fell to mine and lifted it off his leg. "Don't tempt me into doing something both of us will regret."

I was on a high, wielding my sexuality in a way I never had. Something had gotten into me, and I wouldn't stop until something—someone—else got into me.

"And what's that?" I asked, feigning innocence, eyes wide.

He growled, low enough that it was barely audible over the music and conversations in the bar, but it sent a shot of pure lust through me at the primal pull of the sound. "Taking you home and fucking you senseless."

I'd expected an innuendo or another deflection, but his direct and straightforward answer sent a flood of arousal into my panties, and my hand involuntarily squeezed his.

With no conscious thought, a moan left my mouth at his words and I bit my lip, staring at his and wondering how they would feel on my body.

"Jesus, Addy," Landon said. "What's going on?"

It was a good question. I'd never felt this way. Flirting had been fun ever since I gained my curves, but I'd never pushed it so far so fast. I'd always been the good girl.

Something about Landon made me want to be bad.

Before I could doubt myself, I hopped off the stool, put my arm around his neck, and leaned in.

As I'd hoped, Landon didn't pull away. He was only a man.

His lips on mine were surprisingly soft, tempting and pulling me deeper. Even in the space of a few seconds, I could tell he was skilled so far beyond any of the boys I'd ever kissed that comparisons were meaningless.

I moaned and ran my hands over his shoulders as we sank deeper, forgetting where we were. I was lost in his lips and the magic they worked against my own.

By the time he broke the kiss, I was only hanging on to reality by a thread.

LANDON

"My place is around the corner," I said, voice a low growl from the rush of lust coursing through my veins.

I didn't let myself think too hard about how big of a mistake I was making. The decision was already made once the words were out of my mouth, and if I was going to do this, then I wouldn't let second thoughts ruin it.

Addy's eyes fluttered open, and she nodded slowly. "Let's go."

I pulled out my wallet and threw a twenty onto the bar for the whiskey. It was too much, but I wasn't in the mood to wait around for change.

Addy's hand found mine, and her other wrapped around my arm. She pressed her body against mine as if claiming me for all the other women in the bar to see.

We broke into the warm summer air outside, and as soon as we rounded the corner, I pressed her against the wall, wove my hand into her hair, and kissed her deeply.

Addy moaned into my mouth as our tongues slid against each other. She was pinned against the wall, but that didn't stop her from moving her body against mine, shifting her hips to press urgently against mine and letting her legs spread so that my thigh could slide between them and give her something to grind on as our kiss intensified.

Someone behind us cleared his throat, and a chorus of laughs followed. I pulled back from the kiss to look.

Four men in their early twenties stood in a line a few feet away, watching us with cigarettes in hand.

"Not that I don't appreciate the free show, but take her home, bro," said one of the men.

I looked back to Addy. She pulled her dress back down from where it had ridden up and grinned. "I think the guy's got a point."

I shrugged. "Enjoy your night, fellas."

We resumed walking back to the apartment, but this time, instead of holding hands, I put my arm around Addy and let it fall lower and lower until it rested on her ass. It was a tight, firm delight to hold. She leaned into my side, one arm around me and the other on my chest, feeling the muscles bunched under my tight shirt.

"I can't believe this is happening," she said, low, as if it was a thought that had accidentally escaped her lips.

It was the first sign of misgiving she'd shown all night. Her relentless escalation and seduction had left me feeling helpless and beholden to my masculine urges—I'd never been pursued so hard by any woman. Coming from such perfection, it was impossible to resist, no matter how wrong it was.

"We can stop this," I said. "It's really not a good idea. I could lose my job, and who knows what will happen if Nick finds out."

The opportunity to think it through further only brought more reasons to pull back and send Addy home. A night of sex wasn't worth the consequences, no matter how attractive the partner. At the same time, the risk and taboo was what made it so much hotter.

"No!" she exclaimed. "No, I want this. I meant that I never thought this would happen. I used to have such a crush on you. If you pull out now, I'll never forgive you."

I stared at her, dumbfounded. "You had a crush on me? But I'm seven years older than you!"

She blushed. "So? Plenty of girls have crushes on actors and rock stars who are way older than them. It's natural."

I wasn't sure how to feel about that. On one hand, I was flattered, but on the other, it highlighted the age difference between us.

Addy could sense my reticence. She pulled my arm until I stopped, then she leapt at me, wrapping her body around mine in the middle of the sidewalk.

She attacked my mouth with purpose, superheating my blood in moments as her impossibly tight but curvy body pressed against mine and she moaned into my mouth, running her hands across my shoulders and down my back.

Reluctantly, I let myself be drawn back in, unable to resist the lure of the woman in my arms. I let my hands glide down her back until they cupped her ass, and I pulled her tightly against me. The intensity of her attentions sent blood flooding back to my cock, and it hardened in my jeans and pressed against her through the denim and the flimsy material of her dress.

Addy moaned louder, shifting her hips back and forth to rub herself against me, gasping into my mouth at the sensation.

She ran her hands through my hair and used her grip to pull my head to the side, exposing my neck to her greedy mouth.

"Don't think about it," she breathed into my ear. "Let's enjoy ourselves tonight. Just a one-time thing to relieve the tension, and then everything goes back to normal, okay?"

How could I argue with that?

There's no way this could possibly backfire, right?

It didn't matter what the reasoning part of my brain said— the primal, alpha male had awoken from its slumber, and it called the shots.

"Let's get back to the apartment," I growled.

Addy disentangled herself, and we sped down the street. The final half-mile passed by quickly. Neither of us talked, instead trading looks and touches that spoke of the only thing on our minds.

As we walked up to the house, reality intruded. The lights

were on, but Nick was notorious for failing to turn them off when he left. He claimed it prevented break-ins. "Nick might be home," I said. "I need to go in first to check. He was going out with some people from work tonight, and it's still early, but he has work in the morning so he could be back already."

I didn't want to even consider what would happen if my best friend and roommate found me in a compromising situation with his baby sister.

Addy nodded. "Okay. I'll wait here and hide if I hear anyone coming."

I unlocked the door and poked my head in. "Nick, you home, bro?"

My voice echoed through the house, and there was no answer.

I think his shoes are missing. Not at the front door, at least.

The consequences were high enough that I ran through the house, poking my head into every room just to make sure before I went back downstairs and opened the front door.

"We're good."

That's all the notice Addy needed. She rushed inside, but before she could jump at me again, I put out a hand to stop her. She slowed, head tilted to the side as she pouted.

"What?"

I didn't answer verbally, but I shut the door and then backed her against the wall. I took her hands and lifted them above her head, pinning them there with one hand. Addy bit her lip as I let my gaze fully take her in for the first time that night with no shame or attempt to hide it.

"If we're doing this, we're doing it my way. Is that clear?"

As I spoke, I brought my hand to her cheek and let it trace her jaw, then brush down the side of her neck. She shuddered, hips moving against nothing as though she couldn't contain the arousal within her.

She nodded slowly, her eyes wide and innocent. Addy had slept with high school boys. She had no idea what it was like to be with a real man.

To really be fucked.

"Good."

I followed my hand with my lips. Her neck was soft, the flesh sweet. Her breath rasped louder as I expertly used my lips and tongue to create a hot, wet sensation on her body.

Her reactions made me long to go further. I couldn't wait to taste all of her. But there would be time for that later.

I stepped back. "Go up the stairs."

The staircase leading to the second floor was off the entryway, and she obeyed my command without question. I let her get a few steps ahead of me, watching her ass sway from side to side as she climbed the stairs, her black dress barely hiding the swell of her cheeks. The sight set my cock throbbing in my jeans, and I marveled at her tight young body once more.

"Second door on your left," I said once we got to the top of the stairs.

Addy stood in the middle of my room, looking at me expectantly. I had no idea if she'd ever played a submissive role before, but she was a natural at it so far. She knew I was calling the shots.

I touched the stereo system on my desk, and The Weeknd played from the speakers through the room, low and seductive.

"Remove your clothes. As sexy as you can. Show me what you've got."

Addy hesitated, then nodded. She moved to the throbbing beats of the song, gyrating slowly from side to side. Her eyes never left mine until she spun around to show off her backside.

Goddamn.

As she moved her hips and rotated her body, her dress slipped lower and lower, exposing first the delectable breasts that sat high on her chest beneath a simple bra, then the tiny waist before slipping past her wide hips and perfect ass.

Addy wore only a tiny, matching black bra and panty underneath the dress.

"Like what you see?"

That sultry voice was back, the one she'd used when whispering in my ear at the bar, asking me to guess who covered my eyes.

"I don't think it would be possible not to," I said honestly. "You are a dream, Addy. Although there's still more left to see."

In response to my words, she unhooked her bra from the front clasp, then let it fall to my floor.

She teased me for almost the length of an entire song, letting me catch glimpses of the bottoms and sides of her breasts but never the full view, driving me crazy. I was about to order her to drop her arms when she finally did it herself.

"Wow," I breathed.

I couldn't muster anything else in the moment, and it wasn't necessary. She could see the lust in my eyes, and she gave me an alluring look as she hooked her thumbs in her panties, continuing the tease as she lowered them enough to show her neatly trimmed strip of pubic hair before pulling them back up.

She turned around and repeated the move from the rear, bending in half at the waist and peeling the panties down until they just barely remained in place over her pussy.

"Goddamn it, Addy," I said in a primal growl. "You are really going to get it."

"Good," she said, her own voice husky. "That's what I want. You wouldn't believe how wet you've gotten me."

I could believe it. I could see the way her panties glistened.

"Take those off, and then come here," I said. "Your next task is to undress me."

2
ADELINE

I had considered myself experienced for a high school girl coming to college. Not as much as the few girls who seemingly slept with every guy at school, but enough to know what I was doing.

In the few dozen times I'd had sex, nothing came close to the experience so far with Landon, and he was still clothed. The way he ordered me around, exercising complete control over my body and my actions, sent me spiraling into a sodden, dripping mess. I'd never been more wet.

It made me want to be a wanton slut for him. I just wanted to please him more than anything in the world.

Being naked in front of my adolescent crush was a huge rush. He could see all of me, and he wasn't shy about taking advantage of that fact. Like any woman, I had insecurities about my body, but they fell away under the voracious look in his eyes.

I walked to him, eager to feel those muscles with no clothes in the way and even more eager to see what had made such an impressive bulge in his jeans at the bar. I was desperate to feel it, explore it, and please it.

If this was only going to be a one night stand, I wanted to blow Landon's mind. I needed to be the best he's ever had and ever would have. He would dream of me for the rest of his life.

First things first. I need to get him naked.

When I reached him, I wrapped my arms and one leg around him, pressing my nubile body into his, letting him feel my curves against him. At the same time, I could feel the hard muscles under his clothes, his body so much stronger and more developed than the boys I'd been with.

With a slow, steady motion, I dragged my body down his, dropping an inch at a time until my knee was on the ground and my face pressed against his crotch. His hard cock strained against the fabric, and I kissed it as I slid my hands up under his shirt.

I reversed the movement, climbing to my feet in a sinuous motion, taking his shirt up and off his head as I went, revealing the taut abs and hard-packed chest that filled his shirt so well.

I kissed his chest, running my hands over his abs, marveling at the hard muscle and how perfect it was. As I worshipped his torso, my hands fell to his belt, pulling it loose before unbuttoning his jeans. Sending those to the floor, the only thing that remained was his boxer briefs.

Landon had stood impassively this entire time, moving to assist me when necessary but otherwise letting me caress and play with his body, exploring it and satisfying myself. He gasped with a low groan as my hands played over the front of his underwear, tracing the outline of his cock, covering it with my palms and feeling its impressive length.

It wasn't all for his pleasure. Just feeling his member let me imagine what it would be like to take it into my hands for real, how it would feel to try to take it into my mouth, and what it would feel like when he pushed it inside me.

I sank to my knees in front of Landon. It felt like the proper place to be, considering he had been ordering me around this entire time. He was the master tonight, and I was here to please him. Besides, I wanted to be as close as possible when I saw it for the first time.

I tugged on his waistband, taking my time, going slowly so I could relish the moment. It was tortuous in the best possible way, building the anticipation for the reveal.

By the time Landon's cock sprang free of his boxer briefs, I was salivating. The shaft appeared first, bent down with the briefs, and it kept going and going and going until it finally burst free and almost hit me in the face. It came to a rest in front of me, standing proud of his body, and it was so long and thick that I gasped at the sight as my pussy clenched.

"Oh, my God," I breathed. I stared at it, reverent, until I couldn't take it any longer. My hands rose almost of their own accord and wrapped loosely around the shaft. It filled them far more than any other dick I'd ever held.

Landon's groan reminded me that the monster was attached

to an actual person.

"How do you avoid killing girls with this thing?" I asked in wonder. "I think you might split me in half!"

He looked down, his eyes hazy with lust. "You'll just have to trust me."

I wasn't going to back down now.

The goal of being the best Landon's ever had was still forefront in my mind, and I knew one of the best ways to achieve that.

I eyed the cock in my hand, sizing it up, and then brought my head forward to give it a big lick on the underside. It jumped in my hand, and the groan that rolled through his body was music to my ears.

Reading about sex was one of my favorite pastimes—I'd progressed far beyond *Cosmo* a long time ago. By most accounts, enthusiasm was the most important factor in what made a blowjob great.

That wasn't an issue.

I licked, sucked, and wrapped my hands around his member as if my life depended on it. It gave me as much pleasure as it gave Landon, and my pussy only got wetter the longer I spent working over his cock and the louder the groans I coaxed from his body.

It was such a wonder to heft and play with, and I didn't have to feign my need for it.

Landon's reactions grew stronger and more forceful, and his hands fell to the back of my head—not pushing, but letting me know he was in charge no matter how weak I made his knees.

I could sense how close he was getting, feeling the little shakes and vibrations that rolled through his body and signaled his impending climax. Before they could reach a peak, his hands in my hair tightened and pulled me off him. I strained forward to finish him, but he was too strong.

"Not yet," he growled. If his voice had been primal before, it was downright animalistic now, and the sound of his naked desire tore through my body and made me weak.

Landon bent over and wrapped his arms around me, pulling me off the ground as though I were as light as a feather, holding me in his arms for only as long as it took to throw me onto the bed.

He wasn't far behind, prowling onto the bed like a lion on the hunt, and I was his prey.

All it took was a little nudge on the inside of my thighs, and then he was over top of me, breathing over my hot sex, intimidating in his nearness.

"You're gorgeous," Landon said. "I can't wait to taste you. But I have a lot of teasing to do before that happens."

It sounded delightful and harrowing at the same time. I'd already been teased enough by serving him, and all I wanted was to feel his mouth on my pussy.

"Come on, Landon. I can't wait any longer. I'm so wet for you."

He kissed the inside of my thigh, only inches away from my lips. "I can see that."

I flushed, then gasped as he kissed even closer to his goal. "Yes..."

The next moment, his fingers dug into the flesh of my thigh and dragged down toward my knee, his mouth following.

For the next twenty minutes, Landon put my body through an experience unlike any I'd ever had. All the boys I'd had sex with in high school were too eager to rush into the main event. Foreplay had been a half-hearted fingering, and maybe a minute of oral if I was lucky. Landon took longer savoring my body than the longest sexual encounter I'd had.

I didn't think I could get hornier and more ready than I'd been kneeling before him, but I'd been wrong. So incredibly, delightfully wrong.

"Please, Landon, please taste me," I said. "I need to feel it. You're driving me crazy."

I wasn't exaggerating. Pulses of sensation sparked and tingled across the surface of my skin like I was hooked up to a live wire. I'd never been this close to orgasm without anyone touching me directly before—it felt like I could almost get there just from Landon's breath on me and the way he made love to the sensitive skin on my upper hip.

He looked up at me, his mouth twisted into a sly smile. "That's a good start, but you need to work on your begging. Give me no other choice than to lick you."

"I need it so badly. Please make me come, Landon, please. I'll do anything you want, anything at all. I just need to feel your mouth on me."

His mouth hovered above my pussy. I wanted so much to lift my hips up to his mouth, but I trembled as I held myself back. I'd promised to do things his way.

"Call me sir," he said, so close that even if I'd been blind and deaf, I could have felt his words and the way his low voice vibrated against me.

"Please, sir," I whimpered, breathless. "I'm yours. Take me."

The moment his tongue dropped to my delicate skin, I exploded.

His skillful mastery of my body, building me up and making it impossible to think of anything outside of the moment, led to the most intense climax of my life with the barest of touches. My clit was throbbing from my arousal and the lack of contact, and as soon as his tongue gave it the gentlest of caresses, it shuddered and sent a shockwave through my body.

"Oh, God," I said under my breath, barely able to even get the words out. As Landon increased his pressure and my orgasm blossomed into its full glory, I got louder. "Oh, fuck! Landon, sir, oh, my God! Yes, keep doing that. Oh, fuck!"

Words failed me then, my brain devoted to luxuriating in the pleasure that ran through my body and left me unable to think of anything else. It built in my core, reaching a crescendo and pulsing from there throughout the rest of my body, branching down my limbs and out to my fingertips, leaving them tingling as I thrashed on the bed.

Waves swelled and burst forth through my nerves, slowly losing intensity as I came down from the stratospheric heights my brother's best friend had sent me.

I lay back, enjoying the aftershocks as Landon stretched out beside me and kissed my neck.

"That was incredible," I said, pulling him to me and kissing him. He tasted like me, and it wasn't long before his skilled mouth had me ready for more.

He'd already destroyed all of my expectations for what sex could be, and his cock hadn't even come close to my pussy. I needed to do the same thing to him.

Taking the initiative, I pushed Landon onto his back and slid on top of him.

LANDON

Addy's soft skin felt incredible as she straddled me while keeping her body pressed as fully against mine as she could.

My best friend's little sister had come on my tongue, writhing and twisting in the sexiest way I'd ever seen. It made me harder than I even wanted to admit to myself, and for a moment, I considered ending things there before we crossed the final line.

She slid further down and shifted her hips, settling into place on top of me, bringing her pussy into full contact with my rock-hard cock.

I groaned, and her eyes fluttered at the contact that felt so right physically but so wrong at the same time.

That line of thinking died as soon as Addy pressed her pussy against my cock. She shifted her hips, spreading her wetness along my shaft, marking her territory and making us both breathless from the slippery ecstasy of the contact.

"Addy," I groaned, putting my hands on her hips, feeling the way she rocked on top of me. "This feels great, but I should grab a condom."

She ground harder against me. "I really don't want to stop this long enough to do that, sir, and I hate the feeling. I trust you if you trust me."

It was a bad idea for many reasons. But the way she pressed her body against mine and gave a breathy moan into my ear destroyed any chance at using logic.

"I want to feel you, sir," she whispered, accompanied by another groan. "I need you inside me."

I didn't resist as she lifted off me enough to reach between us and grab hold of my cock. Addy gasped as she pushed against the head, impaling herself on my manhood and forcing it a few inches inside her.

"Holy shit," she said, eyes wide as she looked into mine. "You feel incredible."

She hovered there for a moment before sinking further down, her pussy clenching around my cock as an expression halfway between pleasure and determination crossed her face.

"Almost there, Princess," I said before gripping her hips and lifting my own to drive my shaft to the hilt inside her.

"Oh!" Addy's eyes rolled into the back of her head and she bit her lip as I bottomed out inside her.

I added a growl as I adjusted to the intense, tight heat wrapped around me.

The lithe teenager rocked on top of me, small movements

that gave each of us almost unbearable pleasure. After a couple of hours of anticipation from meeting at the bar to this moment, I was almost ready to burst as soon as she sank on top of me. I fought it back ruthlessly, determined to give her the experience of her life.

"God, sir," she said, eyes still only halfway open as she rode me. "This is insane."

It was. In many ways. And that's what made it the hottest sex of my life.

"It is. Your tight pussy feels so good around my cock. Ride me nice and slow."

Addy obeyed, shuddering at the bottom of each thrust as she went.

It felt incredible, but I knew I could make her feel even better.

D.G. Whiskey

ADELINE

Landon's cock felt almost too big inside me. It left me teetering on the edge of sanity, one hard thrust away from losing control.

He gave that to me.

His big, strong hands held tight to my hips, guiding my motions as I rode him and drove his cock deep inside me time and time again. After a few dozen thrusts, he took over.

Using long, smooth strokes, Landon pushed up into me from below.

When his hand slipped up past my breasts and curled loosely around my throat, I nearly passed out from the intensity of the response it engendered in my body. Landon's fingers tightened. It wasn't enough to cut off my air, but I felt wholly within his power in that moment.

Being controlled like that was hotter than anything I'd ever felt, and that was even before accounting for the way he split me open with his member, forcing my pussy to spasm around him and driving me toward delirium with his thrusts.

My eyes rolled back into my head and I let him take total control, giving myself over to the pleasure that swept over me.

Landon used his powerful hands, one on my neck and one around my waist, to roll us over until I was on my back and his powerful frame covered mine. His shoulders were hard boulders beneath my hands, the muscles straining and flexing as he powered our ecstasy.

I'm actually fucking Landon Fraser. I can't believe it's finally happening.

If I were being honest with myself, I wasn't fucking Landon. *He* was fucking *me*.

The realization of an adolescent fantasy doubled the intensity of the moment, and I fought to commit every touch, every breath to memory.

"That's it," he grunted into my ear. "Take my cock, Princess. I want you to come for me."

His command and the hand around my neck left no doubt. I was his, and it took me over the edge. I soon lost any sense of volume control as the overwhelming sensations enveloped me and carried me to incredible heights. My climax was intensified and lengthened by the way Landon continued to fuck me through my peak, refusing to let me rest and bringing my pleasure to a greater pinnacle than I thought possible.

Five seconds before it would have become too much for my sensitive post-orgasm body to handle, Landon slowed his pace and pressed fully inside me.

"Did you finish?" I asked.

"Not yet. I'm nowhere near finished with you, Princess."

His new pet name for me was driving me crazy.

"How do you have that much control?" I stopped short of mentioning my previous partners, but I could see by the look in his eyes that he knew I was comparing him to others. And that he was winning.

He grinned. "Maturity."

Somehow, his cock pulsed, the momentarily swollen girth taking my breath away.

"Oh!" I said. "What did you just do?"

He did it again, his manhood growing bigger and firmer, this time for a few seconds.

"Trade secret."

I was past the overly sensitive part of my climax, but his cock still felt so good. I rocked my hips underneath him until he got the hint and moved in long, glacially slow strokes.

"Oh, my God, Landon," I moaned, reveling in the luxurious feel of this moment, so different from the impassioned pounding I'd just received.

The sound of the bedroom door opening jolted me out of my indulgent haze, and I instinctively turned my face away from the door.

My brother's voice made the interruption even worse.

"Hey, Landon, you ready for your big day tomorrow? Oh,

I'm sorry. Didn't realize you had a girl in here."

I couldn't see my brother with my face buried in Landon's shoulder, but I could hear the sarcasm in his voice.

"Jesus, Nick, get out of here!" Landon growled from on top of me. His body hid most of mine, but he was bare-ass naked with no cover.

"Just wanted to wish you good luck on your lecture tomorrow if I don't see you in the morning." Nick didn't seem concerned that he was talking to his nude roommate while said roommate's cock was buried in a girl—who happened to be his sister.

Landon shook his head. "Fine, thanks. Come on, man, leave us alone."

"You won't introduce me?"

I'd heard Nick and Landon tease each other constantly growing up. Somehow, it didn't surprise me that they would be so nonchalant about a situation like this. They'd go to any lengths to annoy and make the other uncomfortable.

Landon grabbed something from his bedside table and threw it at the door. "Scram, man!"

"Okay, okay."

The door closed with a soft click.

Landon pulled up and we looked at each other.

"That was close," I said, a bare whisper all I dared utter.

"Yeah. We have this thing where we try to make the other uncomfortable if they're having sex. I can't believe I forgot to lock the door."

Silence reigned for a few seconds as the close call sank in. Nick had literally seen us fucking, and only luck had hidden my identity from him.

"We shouldn't be doing this," Landon said, but his manhood remained deep inside me.

I wrapped my legs around him, making sure he couldn't leave. "Nothing's changed. One night, right? We shouldn't waste it."

I was drunk on him, and it didn't matter what the correct decision was. I knew what I wanted.

Before Landon could open his mouth to say anything else, I rolled my hips against him, grinding the head of his cock against the depths of my pussy, forcing him to grunt.

"That's not fair."

I smiled up at him and did it again. "What are you going to do about it, sir?"

That relit the fire inside his eyes, the one that had raged with intensity all night. With a powerful move, he drew his hips back until the head of his cock remained only just inside my entrance.

I whimpered at the sudden absence.

"I will take what I want from you, Princess. And you will like it."

With that, his hips slammed back into mine and took my breath away. I gasped and moaned at the sudden intrusion, and Landon took up a rhythm of deep, powerful thrusts that quickly built my pleasure.

Landon's hand covered my mouth, muffling the screams that threatened to give us away to my brother. His eyes bored into mine, commanding me without words, telling me I was his.

This time, our pleasure crescendoed together, Landon's own grunts signaling his need. When I lost myself in the torrent of pleasure he unleashed through my body, the feeling of him coming within me fed and grew it even further.

He held me in his arms as our breathing slowed, regaining our composure.

"Wow," I said. "That will be hard to top."

Again, my words summoned that cocky grin to his face. "Good luck with that."

He rolled off me, and I mourned the loss until he pulled me close, setting my head on his chest. It was the most comfortable and satisfied I'd ever been.

"Should I go?" I didn't want to, but we had a deal. One night only.

Landon didn't answer for a few moments. "I think I still hear Nick moving around downstairs. We can't risk it. Are you okay with staying here tonight?"

"Of course."

He didn't have to ask twice. I'd take as much of him as I could get. In fact, this would give me an opportunity to make an even better lasting impression on him.

With every second that passed since the best sex of my life, I grew more and more sure—there was no chance I would let this be just a one-night stand.

D.G. Whiskey

3
LANDON

Hazy memories of a nubile body pressed against mine and bursts of insistent pleasure filtered through my mind. The fleeting images scattered before my waking consciousness, chased away by the morning.

One thing remained, and that was the intense pleasure around my cock. It was hot and wet, making me groan before I could even figure out what was going on.

It stopped.

"Good morning, sir."

Then Addy's warm mouth enveloped my manhood once more, and I groaned as I looked down to see her brunette locks tied back in a messy bun, giving me a perfect view as she took me between her lips and used her hands to wrap around the base.

She moaned, the vibrations rumbling through my shaft and spreading through my body. It felt amazing, but what was even better was how enthusiastic and turned on she was.

She must have been doing that for a while before I woke up.

I was already close to coming, and Addy sucked me like a woman possessed. Before long, she coaxed my body through a burst of brilliant energy.

"Fuck, Princess!" I kept my voice low, aware of Nick moving around in the hall.

She took all of my load in her mouth, her throat swallowing around the tip of my cock, the pressure making my thigh muscles jump.

Addy pulled off me and crawled up my body, settling in next to me, folding her arms on my chest and setting her chin on them. "I hope you enjoyed your wake-up call."

"I think you got direct evidence of that."

Even as I spoke, worry pulled at my mind.

Does this break our one-night rule?

I hadn't expected sex with Addy to be this good. Anything extra we did was playing with fire—it was addicting, and I couldn't say no when she woke me up like that.

"I love your taste, sir," Addy said with a cheeky smile.

I shouldn't have taught her to say that.

She didn't say sir in a serious way like she had last night, but with an impudent sparkle in her eyes.

"Sounds like we've got a mutual appreciation society starting here because last night, I was tempted to tie you down and eat you until sunrise. In fact, I need to return the favor."

Addy put her finger on my lips and shook her head. "Nuh,

uh. That was a treat. You'll just have to owe me one."

Owe her one? That's a dangerous attitude to have.

She rolled off me and sprang out of bed before I could convince her otherwise. I watched as she pulled her underwear on with brisk efficiency, unable to peel my eyes away from her curves. It would be the last time I ever saw them this way, and I didn't want to forget.

"You're in a rush," I noted.

It made sense. She shouldn't have even stayed overnight, but Nick's presence hadn't given us a choice.

"First day of school today," Addy said with a wink. "Got lots of preparation to do before classes. Can't make a poor impression on my first day of Harvard."

That's right. She's a student at the school.

Somehow, that detail had almost passed me by, lost behind my concern over her status as Nick's little sister. The school's policies didn't allow professors to have sex with students. I had only just finished my PhD and was incredibly lucky to be hired as an assistant professor—if anyone in the administration found out about my night with Addy, I could lose my job.

"Wise lady," I said, following her out of bed as she wiggled back into her black dress. I threw on a pair of sweatpants. The shower started in the bathroom. "Good timing, too. Sounds like Nick's in the shower, so you've got a chance to sneak out."

I ushered her to the front door. "Addy, this was… great. But we can't do it again, okay?"

It wasn't what I wanted. What I wanted was to ravish her tight body every hour of every day, but there were too many reasons that was a bad idea. Even doing it once was bad enough.

Addy's lips moved to the side as she pursed them, but she nodded. "That's what we agreed on." Then she bounced up on her toes and gave me a peck on the lips. She winked. "I'll see you later. I hope you enjoy your first class, sir."

Her final word sent a pulse of blood to my manhood, her voice turning sultry and sexy as she stared into my eyes and then turned to go.

Jesus. She shouldn't be able to cause that big of a reaction with a single word.

I walked back upstairs in a daze, and by the time I got there, Nick was exiting the bathroom with a towel around his waist.

"Oh, hey man. Nice score last night. Didn't see much of that chick, but she looked hot as fuck."

Part of me was amused at Nick unknowingly complimenting his sister's looks, but the majority was ashamed at betraying my best friend's trust as I had.

"Um, thanks. We had a good time."

"I bet. You pick her up at the bar last night?"

More like she picked me up.

"Something like that."

Nick frowned, looking at my face. My stomach lurched.

He knows something's wrong.

"You're being quiet. Nervous about your first lecture? Why

don't we go out for dinner tonight with Adeline? I told her we'd show her around town."

I almost choked on my tongue but was able to turn it into a cough. "Addy? Dinner?"

"Yeah, it's no big deal. If your lecture goes well, then we'll celebrate, and if not, then we'll drink away our sorrows."

There was no way I wanted to sit at the same table as the siblings the night after I showed her how real men fucked. I also couldn't think of a good excuse not to.

"That... sounds good, I guess."

Nick nodded and slapped my shoulder. "There you go. I'll need your help keeping the guys off her. You haven't seen her in years, but that girl grew up, and she knows it. I want her to have fun at college, just not that much fun, you know what I mean?"

I winced. "I know exactly what you mean."

"Good. I've got to jet to work, but we'll figure out details for dinner later."

The conversation left me more to think about than I wanted. Thoughts of Addy's curved lips and curvaceous body wouldn't leave me alone as I showered and got ready for work. I may as well have been a robot for the amount of conscious attention I paid the world around me until I arrived at the lecture hall.

Luckily, this was the first lecture of the day for the hall, so I didn't have to wait for the previous class to leave before going in and getting things set up. It was just as well, because the computer stubbornly refused to recognize my slides. Instead of greeting my students as they came in the door as I intended, I hunched behind the computer, running through every fix I could think of until it finally, miraculously started working.

The volume in the room had steadily risen as students sat and chatted with their friends and neighbors, waiting for class to start.

Okay, good to go. Only a minute late. That's not too bad.

The last few students straggled in as I stood and gave the room a quick scan. I cleared my throat.

It was too loud for any but the students in the first row to hear, so I spoke up. "Excuse me, ladies and gentlemen, it's time to start."

This time, the noise lowered and gradually tapered off as students either heard me and turned toward the front or noticed those who had.

"My name is Landon Fraser, and I'm an assistant professor of business economics at Harvard. My area of research is applying machine learning techniques to optimize corporate finance policies." I looked more carefully at the mass of students arrayed before me as I spoke, trying to learn the faces of the students I would be teaching for the next four months.

"I only just finished my PhD last year, so it was not all that long ago that I sat where you are now, learning the basics of macroeconomics. It was this class, in particular, that gave me a passion for economics and persuaded me to change from software engineering to economics. I…"

I trailed off at the sight of the gorgeous brunette in the fifth row.

Addy? What the hell is she doing here?

She was dressed in a short skirt and a tight top, her legs crossed demurely as she grinned at my reaction. Only at a murmur from the back of the room did I realize that I'd trailed off in the middle of my speech and was staring at Addy.

"I'm sorry, I lost track of where I was going for a second. I hope that this class is as useful and inspiring to you as it was to me. Now, here is the syllabus. I hope at least some of you have gone on the course website and looked at it already."

I flashed up the pertinent slide, unable to resist shooting another look at Addy. For the next twenty minutes, I struggled to keep my eyes off her, and from the smirk on her face every time I failed, she knew it.

She looks way too good. It's not fair that Nick's little sister had to be that good-looking and come to Harvard. And why the hell is she sitting in my class?

As I introduced the class's teaching assistants and let them say a few things about themselves, my eyes slipped over to the center of the fifth row.

Addy wasn't paying attention to the teaching assistants. Her eyes were on me—they had been the entire time, even when slides were on the screen.

Our gazes locked, and she bit her lip. Then she shifted, uncrossing her legs and letting them drift open.

Oh, my god.

My eyes were level with Addy's knees where she sat in the fifth row. And once she spread them, they were level with another part of her anatomy—and she wasn't wearing any panties.

My mouth dropped, and I was even more grateful for the lectern. It had provided a solid anchor to give me confidence during the lecture, but now it served in another way—hiding the massive erection that had formed in a matter of seconds and stuck down the leg of my pants.

I fought to tear my eyes away, but they were drawn as if by a powerful magnet. It didn't help that she was so turned on that I could see it.

ADELINE

If Landon's face was any indication, there wasn't any more blood left to power his brain. His cheeks flamed, and he shifted behind the lectern, gripping it with both hands.

The thrill inside me was electric. I'd never let myself do anything so freeing, so... *slutty* before.

Except maybe coming onto him last night and going home with him.

I was so turned on, and all I wanted was for his hands to be gripping me instead of the inanimate hunk of wood in front of him.

The third and final teaching assistant finished speaking, and most of the eyes in the room shifted back to Landon. He had composed himself impressively well, and if I hadn't known exactly what I'd done to him, it would have been hard to tell.

"Thank you very much, Josie. Now, today is your first day of classes, and I'm sure you don't want to be bogged down with too much information so soon. I think what we've covered today outlining the layout of the course is enough for now, and we will start right in on the first macroeconomics lecture next class. Welcome to Harvard, everybody."

It was only half an hour into class, but none of the students would think twice about being dismissed early. I crossed my legs again as the room exploded with activity, students packing up their notebooks and hurrying out as though granted a reprieve from hell.

Even the teaching assistants didn't stick around for long, and soon, I was the only one left besides Landon. Since he'd dismissed class so early, there wasn't anyone waiting in the hall for the next class yet.

I wonder if he did that on purpose?

He'd looked so hot at the front of the class, holding forth with authority. I hadn't been sure I would follow through with the plan, but seeing him talk to the class was a bigger turn-on than I could have imagined.

Landon's eyes were fierce, scouring my body as I descended to the front of the room.

"What are you doing here, Addy?"

He didn't sound pleased. I hadn't expected him to, but he could have been a little more welcoming than that.

"I'm just attending my first introduction to macroeconomics class," I said innocently. "Or, I was until the professor let the class out early."

His brow furrowed, and he frowned. "I don't believe it. You're in this class? Why didn't I see you on the roster?"

I tilted my head to the side, trying to keep a smile off my face. "When was the last time you checked? I only transferred in this morning."

He sighed, his eyes closing. "Goddamnit, Addy. This makes everything so much worse. Why would you go and do something like that?"

I didn't see what the big deal was. "Because this is so fun. Won't this be awesome, having me in your class?"

The door to the lecture hall opened, and a grizzled man in a sweater vest entered with a briefcase. He and Landon exchanged nods.

"Professor Adelman. It's a pleasure to see you."

"Ah, Landon. Good first class?" The older man gave me a curious look, and I practiced my innocent face once more.

Landon cleared his throat. "Not bad at all, sir." He shut his laptop and shoved it into his bag, clearing the platform for the other man.

We edged away from Professor Adelman. I leaned in to Landon's ear. "I was wet all day from giving you that blowjob this morning, so I wanted to show you. And then that got me even more wet."

The look on Landon's face was priceless. "Addy, we can't do this… for so many reasons." He spoke in a low, measured voice and glanced to the side to see if the other professor had overheard us. "You agreed it was a one-time thing. I meant that. There are too many repercussions if we get caught."

Chastened, I nodded. I didn't want to get him in trouble, but there was a problem.

His self-control was admirable, but it made me want him even more. He'd fucked me better than I ever knew possible, and it was hard to just let that go.

Not without experiencing it a few more times, at least.

LANDON

I thought getting to the restaurant early would give my heart rate time to come down and give my mind an opportunity to settle itself. I hoped that I wouldn't see Addy's achingly gorgeous body writhing on my sheets every time I closed my eyes.

Instead, it took away any ability to occupy myself, leaving me with nothing but thoughts of her—the way she'd screamed my name, the devilish glint in her eye as she took my cock in her mouth, and how she expertly flashed me in the middle of my first lecture.

"Is this seat taken?"

The woman herself slid into the booth next to me. I'd sat at the edge of the bench so she wouldn't have room to squeeze next to me, but she didn't care. Half of her ass hung over the side, and Addy pressed her body firmly against mine so she wouldn't fall off.

Sighing, I shifted to the side, giving her more space. She

edged over on the bench, following me, maintaining contact.

"Addy…"

"Problem?" Her face turned toward mine, not smiling, but the hints of it were in the corners of her eyes and the tightness of her cheeks.

The fox.

She was determined to ignore any commitment to propriety I forced her to make. It was like dealing with a kitten that listened to my words but then did whatever the hell it wanted anyway.

Addy still wore the short skirt and tight top combo that she'd used to catch and hold my attention in class. I struggled to keep my mind away from wondering if she'd bothered to put any panties on since then.

I didn't respond to her question. There was enough on my plate just trying to avoid getting hard at the thought of her potentially bare pussy within arm's reach and the way her body felt against mine.

I failed.

"Now, aren't you two a sight?" Nick walked up to the table and sat on the other side of the booth, sliding into the middle of the table. "I'm surprised you guys aren't deep in conversation after not seeing each other for so long. Hasn't it been since we left for college, Landon?"

"That's right," I said. "And we've talked plenty. You just caught us at a lull in conversation."

Addy tapped me on the shoulder. "This isn't even the first

time I've seen Landon today! I'm in his macroeconomics class."

Nick guffawed. "No way, really? Oh man, that's priceless. How great is that?"

I sighed. "It's super great. Just terrific."

Addy punched me on the thigh, uncomfortably close to my hard cock. Then she let her hand linger. I tried to bat it away, but she ignored my efforts and I couldn't try harder without it being obvious above the table.

"I can't believe we're all back in the same city," Nick said. "And now that we're all adults, we'll have so much more fun. Especially because Addy isn't such a little brat now."

"A brat, huh?" Addy asked. She gave me a sidelong look. "I'm still plenty bratty. If it's called for."

I had already seen some of that behavior.

"Maybe we'll have to train that out of you," I said.

Nick laughed and missed the way Addy flushed and bit her lip as we met eyes. Her hand squeezed my leg.

"I mean, she's in your class, Landon. You've got to give her good marks, man, and make sure there's no funny business going on with any of the guys there."

"Hey!" Addy kicked her brother under the table, and he flinched. "I'm a grown woman, Nick. And you know I'm smarter than you. I don't need any help with my marks, and as for my love life, you can stay the hell out of it."

"Alright, Addy, jeez. What are you wearing heels for? They hurt."

I stared between them, shocked. Addy had always been impetuous as a child, but Nick had always had the upper hand in every situation purely from the age difference. It didn't look like that was the case anymore.

"I like them," she replied. "They make my ass and legs look great."

That made Nick blanch. "Ugh, gross, Addy. We don't need to hear that."

She rolled her eyes. "I'm not your kid sister anymore, Nick. Now I'm your grown-up, adult sister. And Landon's not related at all. Get with the program."

"Whatever. You'll always be the baby to us, sis. Right, Landon?"

I looked at Addy. I didn't see a baby. I saw a confident young woman with a spark of wit and intelligence in her eyes. "Sure, Nick."

Nick got up. "I need to hit the bathroom. Can you order a beer if the waitress comes by while I'm gone?"

When he left, Addy and I stared at each other. The tension was thick between us, and her hand was still on my leg only inches away from my hardened manhood.

She broke the silence first. "Am I forgiven for my stunt this morning, sir?"

That *sir* caught my attention as it always did, the playful tone of her voice doing nothing to tame the animal caged within me. If we'd been somewhere private, I would have thrown her over the table and had my way with her right there.

I didn't answer her, instead dropping my hand to her thigh, just below the skirt. Her eyes widened as I slid it slowly over the smooth, supple skin underneath the breezy fabric.

She bit her lip as I continued, never stopping, following the same inexorable pace. Her own hand squeezed my leg as I crept closer to her core. A slight gasp left her lips as I reached her pussy, my fingertip grazing the sensitive skin and feeling how slick it was already.

Continuing in the same motion, my finger split her lips and slid inside, surrounded by the wet heat and rippling texture of her walls, pushing deep until it couldn't go any further.

With a single pull against her front wall, I withdrew the finger as slowly as my muscles would allow, letting her pussy grip it for as long as possible before slipping free. She stared into my eyes the entire time, lower lip trembling as she moaned softly, first in pleasure and then in frustration once my finger left her.

I brought my hand up to her face and placed the wet finger against her lips. Obediently, she opened her mouth and let me slide the finger inside. She sucked and twirled her tongue around the finger, eyes flickering closed as she worked.

Once I was satisfied, I took it out.

"Now you're forgiven, Princess."

I turned back to the table just as Nick returned and clambered into his seat. "Has the waitress still not come? Man, what's going on tonight? I'm sorry, Addy, this place usually has much better service."

"That's... Ahem, sorry... That's fine, Nick. Not in any rush." Addy had to clear her throat after her first word barely squeaked out. She glanced at me. "The service is great here."

As if on cue, the barmaid arrived to take orders, and then the three of us rehashed stories from our childhood, interchanged with Nick and I giving Addy pieces of advice about Harvard and Boston.

The entire time, I was wracked with guilt for crossing a line I knew I shouldn't have crossed. It would probably come back to bite me in the ass, but something about Addy was addicting, and I couldn't stop myself.

After the way she'd teased me during lecture that morning, the dark side of me was supremely content at the way Addy squirmed in her seat for the rest of the night, desperately horny and wet and unable to do anything about it.

4
ADELINE

I took a deep breath, steeling my nerves.

With a sharp rap on the oaken door, I crossed the point of no return, unable to back away gracefully.

This isn't like you, Addy. You should really take a step back from this.

I couldn't though. It's like a sex demon had possessed my body and was determined to lead me deep into hedonistic temptation.

"Come," Landon's muffled voice was barely audible through the door.

With another deep breath, I opened the door and put on a more confident and alluring face than I actually felt.

"Wow, it's amazing that you can make me come with just one word," I said with a smile. Landon's eyes had been on his computer screen, but the sound of my voice jerked his head straight to meet my gaze.

He was dressed similarly to his attire for the lecture the day before. The crisp blue shirt and gray herringbone jacket were tailored to his tapered torso and broad shoulders, making him look more like a classy investment banker than a frumpy economics professor. It wasn't fair how hot he looked.

He didn't look like this back in Boulder, I'm positive. He hasn't just improved his body—his style is impeccable.

I'd had a big enough crush on him back then, and now all it took was five seconds in his presence to get flustered.

"Ha. Ha. Good one, Addy." He didn't smile. The way his deep voice toyed with my name had me weak in the knees, but I was disappointed he didn't use the Princess nickname he'd given me. From the look on his face, he wasn't happy to see me. "What are you doing here?"

Landon was doing a remarkably good job of keeping his eyes on my face. I'd worn my favorite pushup bra paired with a low-cut blouse to put my assets on display for him, but he wasn't taking the bait this time.

Oddly, that made me feel even more like a desperate slut than if he'd ogled me.

Why am I doing this? He's said it could cost him his job if we do something and get caught. Am I that big of an asshole? I don't want to earn a reputation on campus in the first week of school.

Then Landon cocked his head to the side, and his raised eyebrow reminded me of the night we'd spent together. *That* was why I was doing this. Because I'd never felt pleasure like that before, and I'd never experienced such a deep, visceral connection to another human being.

As awful of a person as I was for pursuing what I shouldn't want, it felt even worse to simply abandon it and never know what could have been. My entire being screamed at me that there was something special here.

And it's not like he doesn't want it, too. He's never denied how much he wants me. He just has better control than I do.

"I was reading through the syllabus, and I noticed that you're selecting one undergraduate student to help with your research. I want to be that student."

Landon's brows furrowed, and he leaned back in his chair, the material of his suit falling gracefully around his built shoulders. "Look, Addy, it's bad enough you switched into my class. I won't make you my research assistant, too. The whole point of the position is to develop a bright young mind and steer them into a career in economics. It will be a merit-based appointment, and I'll only take the best in the class as my protégé."

I frowned. Maybe I had been playing the ditzy, sex-starved college girl angle too hard. It was hard to stop, though, because it was *so* damn fun. "Do you think I'm stupid, sir?"

He froze.

I walked around his desk and sat down on his side, within easy reach. Leaning over, my cleavage was so close to his eyes that the only way he could avoid looking is if he kept them closed.

From here, I could see the bulge that grew in his pants, and the sight of it emboldened me further.

"I would love to spend more time with you, *sir*. Is that such a bad thing? I think we would both enjoy it. Sir."

As I spoke, I slipped the heel off my left foot and reached it out to his crotch. The movement let my skirt ride up, and once more, I had conveniently "forgotten" to wear panties. Landon's eyes were glued to the junction of my thighs, his dark orbs filled with the fire that signaled his state of mind.

My foot contacted the rod of steel inside his suit pants. The thin fabric offered no real resistance, and Landon groaned as I ran my foot along his length.

The situation lasted only a few seconds before Landon burst into action. He rose to his feet and snatched me off the desk. Before I could adjust to what was happening, he'd turned me around and bent me over his desk until my stomach and chest were flat on the hard surface.

Landon's hand was on my shoulder, the other on my waist, and he leaned in close, his body pressing against mine as his breathing grew harsh in my ear. His voice was a loud whisper.

"Don't make me punish you, Princess. I won't take it easy on you."

His hand on my waist flipped the back of my skirt up and onto my back, exposing my ass and bare pussy for him. His fingers traced the curves of my ass and thighs, lightly dancing along my skin and taking my breath away, but never touching where I needed them most.

My pussy flooded with desire for him, the need to feel his huge member inside me once more. I panted, desperate to moan, to beg, but anxiously aware of all the offices surrounding Landon's and their likely lack of adequate soundproofing.

I needed him so badly, and I squirmed my ass back against him, silently asking for a tongue, or a finger, anything to give me the relief and pleasure just out of reach.

He ignored my movements, continuing with the slow, ruthless tease of my flesh, denying me the glory of his fingers on my pussy.

How much longer is he going to keep this up for?

My heartbeat had gone crazy, thundering in my ears so loudly that I missed the knock at the door. Only Landon's soft curse and the way he hauled me to my feet alerted me of the change in circumstances.

"Professor?"

Oh, shit!

I patted my skirt and ran a hand through my hair as the door to the office opened. One of the teaching assistants from yesterday's lecture stood in the doorway. Her eyes widened as they jumped back and forth between me and Landon.

"Ah, Josie, there you are," Landon said. His voice was rough and raspy, and he sat in his chair. "Adeline was just here for my office hours, but she's leaving now."

I smiled and nodded. There wasn't anything else I could do.

"That's right. I have history class. I'll talk to you later, professor."

Josie's eyes narrowed as she watched me approach and pass her into the hallway beyond. Once free, I heaved a sigh of frustration.

I can't believe she ruined that moment.

Hopefully, nothing worse came out of it.

LANDON

My cock was harder than diamond and big enough that it was impossible to hide while standing. Sitting behind my desk was better, but I'd moved too late—Josie's eyes flicked from my face to the desk and back as she approached.

Shit.

The teaching assistant's face had blushed to a faint rose, and her lower lip trembled. "I'm sorry for interrupting, professor, but I have the application files for the undergraduate research posting ready to go live on the course website. I wanted to check with you before submitting in case you wanted to look through one more time."

That's what she interrupted for?

I fumed inside for only a few moments, then cleared my head. I was still turned on, still way too heated over the way Addy had seduced me. Rather than be upset, I should thank Josie for preventing me from making an even bigger mistake than the ones

I'd already made.

"That's quite all right, Josie. I trust you to put everything together properly. I'll make the announcement in the next lecture and give the students a week to compose their applications before I read through the entries and make my decision."

Josie nodded but didn't turn to go. "Is everything okay, professor?"

Except for my aching erection?

Fighting back another surge of annoyance, I nodded. "Everything's fine, Josie."

She cocked her head to the side. "You know, you're really cute. Definitely the cutest professor on campus. I was so happy when I found out I was assigned to your section for this course."

I blinked, surprised. A question about Addy's presence in my office would have been unwelcome but expected. This was a complete surprise, and I didn't know how to respond.

"Um, Josie…"

"You know, you're kind of a legend around campus with the postgrad women. There are so many stories, and they're all so impressive." Her eyes fell to where I hid my crotch behind my desk.

Seriously?

I'd enjoyed my years in the postgrad ranks, and that included sleeping with several attractive ladies pursuing advanced degrees at Harvard, but I never dreamed it would lead to becoming the subject of gossip.

"I..." *What do I say to that?* "I guess I'm flattered?"

Josie bit her lip. "I'd love to see if all the rumors are true."

I didn't let it show, but inwardly, I shook my head. It was just my luck. I'd had my share of conquests, but this was the second woman to throw herself at me. And thanks to the departmental rules, I wasn't allowed to sleep with either of them.

"Look, Josie, you're a beautiful woman, but Harvard has rules about that kind of thing. Professors cannot sleep with TAs."

Josie pouted. "What about with students?"

I looked at her sharply. What had she assumed had gone on in the office before she came in?

"Not with students either."

An awkward couple of seconds filled the air between us before she shrugged. "Okay, fine. I'll upload the posting, professor. Thank you."

She turned to go.

"Thank you, Josie."

I buried my face in my hands as the door clicked closed behind her.

Being a professor is harder than I thought it would be, but for all different reasons.

LANDON

Ugh. Did he actually use the word "like" two times in one sentence?

I stopped reading the application and flipped it into the trash.

"For fuck's sake," I muttered. "There has to be at least one student who's not a complete moron."

I picked up the next application and got only a quarter of the way down the first page before tossing it.

Maybe I didn't give them enough time to write a proper essay.

The requirements for the applications weren't too onerous. At least, I hadn't thought so. A generic questionnaire and an original essay on my research and possible applications the student thought it could be useful for seemed simple enough a task. It wasn't too much to ask of a student who will be helping with that very same research.

Selecting an undergraduate research assistant was supposed

to be a way to find and identify a prodigy, a young mind capable of great things within the field of economics. Instead, every application so far read like it was written by a brain-dead frat boy with no more critical thought than a monkey flinging poop. A few of the applications even smelled like beer.

At least a monkey knows how to use tools. How did these imbeciles even get into Harvard?

Rifling through the rest of the applications, I caught the name on the one on the bottom—the one that must have been put into the drop box first.

Adeline Hudson.

Part of me wanted to open it and read it right then.

She probably wrote "fuck me" all over the application.

Things between us had cooled over the past couple of weeks. She still came to every lecture looking like she had just finished posing for an Instagram photo, impossibly sexy for a woman who still couldn't legally drink alcohol. Luckily, she hadn't flashed me again or shown up in my office. Every time Nick arranged something with the three of us, I bailed out at the last minute.

I kept her application on the bottom of the pile, resolutely fighting the need to read it. As I read the other five remaining, it whispered to me, stealing my concentration.

Only one of the five had been anywhere close to acceptable, and only barely.

Perhaps I was expecting too much out of a class of first-year macroeconomics students.

There was still one application left.

"Fine. Let's see what you wrote, Addy."

I picked up the application and started reading.

My jaw fell open and kept dropping lower as I read. Several times, I flipped back to the cover page to double-check that Addy's name was still there.

Her essay was a proper dissertation on the potential of technology to disrupt the corporate finance world and included an accurate summation of my published work to date. She even drew a connection between them that I hadn't considered.

What the hell? Did she get another student to write this for her?

It was exactly the type of essay I'd been hoping to see—something that demonstrated advanced levels of data acquisition and analytical thought. I'd expected to see this sort of application, but from one of the male foreign-born students in the class, not the hottie from my hometown.

Is that sexist? Or racist? Or both?

She'd followed the instructions and left her contact information on the cover page. I nearly called her number but decided I didn't want to have this conversation over the phone. Instead, I sent her a simple email to ask if she was on campus and if she had time to meet to discuss her application.

Within two minutes, I had a reply. Addy was on a break between classes and hanging out with friends in the next building over. She could be right there.

Before I could over-think it, I sent the message.

Her knock preceded her head poking through the door. "You wanted to see me?"

"Yes. Please come in and sit down. On the other side of the desk."

She grinned at the subtle reminder of the last time she'd been in the office. With the strut of the supremely confident, she walked to the chair opposite the desk and sat in it. Addy was wearing the most modest clothes I'd seen her in, a simple pair of jeans and t-shirt, but even those couldn't hide her curves and the studied grace of her body.

"I'll come out and say it, Addy. Your application for the research position blew me away."

She smiled. "In a good way?"

"Of course." There was no way she could think anything else. "I just don't know how you could have done it. You weren't even in macroeconomics until the morning before the first lecture, so how could you have read all of my work and been able to write such a comprehensive analysis in such a short period?"

Addy frowned and tapped her knee. "You've been assuming things about me, Landon. Way too many things. There are two different professors teaching macro this term, and I was in the other class. I switched to yours because I thought it would be more fun that way."

That caught me by surprise. "You did?"

"Yes. All through high school, I kept up nearly perfect

marks, and thanks to you, I'd always considered going into economics or business. I sure as hell wasn't going to follow Nick into engineering. I'd read each of your papers as you published them and thought they were brilliant."

I was speechless. "But... I had no idea. I mean, you were always a smart kid growing up, but then you got so... hot."

Her nostrils flared. "And hot girls can't be smart? Is that it?"

"Well, no, of course not." I was sputtering, suddenly realizing what a big hole I'd dug myself into.

"Look, Landon, you may bring out the wanton slut in me, but that's not my identity. It's not even something I've ever experienced before. It was just fun to experiment with, and you made me want it so badly." There was no hesitation in her voice, as though she'd practiced saying these exact words.

I took a deep breath and let it out, looking at the sexy and smart woman in front of me whom I'd unfairly discounted even though she was my best friend's little sister.

"I owe you an apology, Addy. I underestimated you, and that was awful of me. I won't lie. Your application was, far and away, the best I've seen."

Addy tilted her head to the side. "But? I can sense one lurking."

"Whatever is between us has to die. I'll give you the spot if you can swear that you will never try to start anything again. There will already be far too much scrutiny when the youngest professor on campus picks the hottest freshman to help him with his research."

She smiled. "You really think I'm the hottest freshman here?"

I rolled my eyes. "Not the point, Addy."

"Sorry." Her smile became a grin. "My academic career is more important than sex. No matter how unbe-fucking-lievable it was. I just got caught up in being naughty. It won't happen again."

I stood and held out my hand. "Then I'm pleased to offer you the position, Addy."

"Put me in any position you want, sir." Addy cut off my reaction with a wave of her hand and a laugh. "Sorry. Last one, I promise."

5
ADELINE

"God-fucking-damnit."

After a couple of months working closely with Landon, I was used to him swearing under his breath when simulation runs didn't go the way he expected. Today, he was swearing more than usual.

"We'll get it on this next one," I said, putting more encouragement into my voice than I felt and putting my hand on his arm.

He stared at the computer screen as if he could melt the offending hardware with the power of his mind. "Shut up, Addy. We're fucked."

I shied away from him, shocked.

Landon could get moody when things weren't going his way, but he'd *never* taken it out on me. Our relationship had grown from one of constant seduction and temptation to the close, cordial relationship between close colleagues.

It was incredible to have such a close, inside look at the man who still made my heart pound, but it was that much more of a struggle to keep my emotions bottled up.

His snapped temper sent those emotions flaring, and I took a deep breath to hold back an automatic jibe in response. The project had started well, but the past few weeks had been a disaster, Landon's computer models churning out nonsensical data more often than useful information. The department had already warned him he had limited time left to right the ship.

"It's not that bad," I said after crunching a few numbers. "The GDP estimates are off, sure, and the trading volume is way lower than we expected, but the target price looks bang on."

"Meaningless," he said. "I need a solid data set for the grant application deadline tomorrow morning, and this is garbage. Half the variables are all over the place."

He wasn't in the mood to be soothed.

Well, that's just fine. He can be angry all he wants, but that won't solve anything.

I lapsed into silence beside Landon, giving up on trying to cheer him.

We sat in the research lab used by the economics department. It was a cozy space, just a dozen work stations set up with access to the powerful servers that ran simulations. Over the past two months, I'd spent more time in here with Landon than any other room on campus except for my dorm room. It was the time I looked forward to the most in my day—working so closely with such a brilliant mind contained within such a sexy body.

"Professor?" A head poked into the room through the lab's door. It was Josie. "Do you need help with anything? I've finished marking the last of the midterms."

Landon shook his head. "You'll just get in the way, Josie. Get out of here."

Eyes wide, the teaching assistant retreated, and the door slammed shut behind her.

"Landon!" I hit his shoulder. "What the hell do you think you're doing? Just because the project is going through a rough patch doesn't mean that you have the right to be such a big dick to everyone."

After an initial rough patch, I'd grown to like Josie. The short blonde was of a similar spirit—intelligent but with a troublemaker's soul. She'd been rude for the first week or two of my research position, but we bonded over our love of running.

Before Landon could respond to the berating I gave him, the door opened again, and this time, a scrawny male with long hair stood in the doorway.

Oh shit. I forgot about Brody.

The disheveled young man held up a book. "Are you ready to go, Adeline?"

Landon groaned beside me. "Who the fuck is this, now?"

Brody stuttered. "Um, sorry, hi, I'm Brody. I was supposed to pick up Adeline for dinner."

I opened my mouth to interject, but Landon was too fast.

"How about you fuck off, Brody? We have more important things to do than your dinner. Why don't you come back when your balls drop?"

The freshman's mouth worked but no sound came out. Instead, he shot Landon a terrified look and backed out of the lab. If he'd been an animal, his tail would have been between his legs.

"Landon!" I said, aghast. "What the fuck is wrong with you?"

He gritted his teeth and the muscles jumped in his chiseled jaw. "Are you dating that buffoon?"

His confrontational attitude put my back up, and I crossed my arms. "I can do whatever I want, Landon."

As if I could fuck a guy my age after knowing what Landon can do. He's ruined me for other men.

Still, I couldn't tell him that.

We stared at each other, the silence ticking on in a dangerous showdown. It felt like waiting to see if an alpha predator would strike, frozen in hopes it would pass on by.

"Fine," I said, unable to take the staring contest any longer. "Brody is just a friend from class. We were supposed to get food and study tonight. I didn't know putting together this application would take so long. I guess he came to find me when I didn't show up at the front of the building. I do have other classes and a life outside of this research."

Landon's breathing had mellowed out and the deadly fire in his eyes dampened. "I'm sorry, Addy. I was out of line. You can

76

obviously do whatever and date whomever you want."

"That's where you're wrong. I can't date the person I want."

My heart jumped at my boldness. I'd said it without thinking—neither of us had even mentioned the searing heat between us over the past two months. The intense attraction had never faded, and we never talked about it, but it was there in the loaded looks, the friendly touches.

Landon looked into my eyes for a few seconds, then turned back to the workstation. He keyed in the initial conditions for the next simulation, refusing to address my words. They lingered on the air, surrounding us.

For the next several hours, we continued to run simulations and gather the data needed for the grant application, layers of tension woven between us—the stress of needing to get work done and the sensual spark that had reignited. Every time I leaned over Landon to point something out or he touched my elbow to get my attention, my skin was on fire, prickling from the proximity.

The light faded outside the windows, and my stomach grumbled embarrassingly loudly.

Landon tore his attention from the screen to look at me. "Was that your stomach?"

My cheeks flushed. "I think so…"

He looked at the time and swore again. "Jesus. How did it get so late? And I prevented you from getting your dinner. You must be starving."

"I'm not that—" Another growl cut me off.

My eyes widened, and Landon laughed at my expression. Chagrined but resigned to the situation, I joined him, laughing ruefully.

"I guess I am pretty hungry."

Once I let it take my attention, I was shocked at how ravenous I was. My mind had been so preoccupied with the data in front of me and the man beside me that the emptiness of my stomach had been the least of my priorities.

"Why don't we go to mine and Nick's? I have a secure connection to the server from there, and we can finish things up after grabbing dinner. We can even call Nick and get him to order something for the three of us so it'll be ready when we get there."

I didn't want Nick there as a buffer between me and Landon, but I understood why Landon had suggested it. It was better than not spending more time with him.

"Let's do it."

LANDON

Tin foil wrappers and plastic takeout containers littered the table, the remnants of a decimated Indian feast. Addy and I were on the couch, laptop in my lap, waiting for the latest simulation to run.

Soft snores from the La-Z-Boy across the room had begun a few minutes ago and only grew louder.

Addy sighed. "I should get Nick to bed."

The three of us had puzzled over the model's inaccuracies while eating dinner. Nick's expertise as a software engineer was invaluable, and it was only through his suggestion that I had begun this avenue of research for my postgrad. As the hours stretched on, he faded rapidly. Working a start-up schedule meant that he woke early, worked late, and never got enough sleep.

With light steps, Addy crossed the room and shook her brother lightly on the arm. Her tight yoga pants stretched across her firm, round cheeks, and I got an eyeful—I couldn't resist.

"Nick?"

He groaned and shifted, and she pushed him harder until the snoring stopped.

"Wha'?"

"Go to sleep, Nick. We've got it from here."

My best friend blinked wearily, looking around the room as if surprised not to be in his own bed already.

"Thanks, Addy. 'Night, you two."

He rolled off the chair and stumbled through the hall to the stairs like a zombie.

"You know, I don't think he even fully woke up," I said, watching him go. It wasn't the first time I had to deal with Nick's ability to pass out anywhere. He was the best sleeper I knew.

Addy grinned as she walked back across the room. "There's no chance he'll remember that in the morning. It'll be like an alien just transported him to bed."

Goddamn, she looks sexy.

The late hour had taken Nick out, but she was still going strong. There was an inner strength to Addy that drew me, like she could take on the world. It had been hard enough to control myself over the past couple of months, but the way she'd pressed against my side all night had tested my self-control like nothing else. Only Nick's presence had prevented me from snapping.

Her smile faded as she curled up and looked at the screen. "Again?"

I looked at the results of the simulation and sighed. "It's looking like we won't have enough quality data to include with the proposal. The project will get canceled."

"Bullshit," Addy said, shaking her head. "We have plenty."

I didn't bother responding. Addy's optimism was a refreshing change from the bleakness of my own thoughts. I'd staked my entire academic career and reputation on this research, promising to break the mold of conventional economics and usher in a new era of data-driven corporate policy. Now, it looked like I would be proven a fool in front of the entire department.

There was nothing preventing me from starting over and researching something else, but I didn't know where to start.

"We'll just have to give up on the grant and try fixing the model later," I said. "It's late, and there's no way we're getting there tonight. If we're lucky, then maybe we can figure out what's wrong before the entire program gets the axe from lack of funding."

Addy put her hand on my forearm. It was soft and hot, oddly distracting. "I won't let you give up on this, Landon. It's only eleven o'clock. We still have nine hours before the application is due. I know we're on the right track. I can feel it. There's just something we're missing."

"We can't do any more tonight. Even if we find a flaw, there may be others, and we won't have the time to run all the simulations. Tomorrow, we'll go through everything with a magnifying glass and see what we can turn up."

Even that was more of a hope than I truly felt. The simulations had been going off the rails for weeks, and we'd spent countless hours trying to find the reason. It was time to chuck it out the window and start fresh.

Addy pursed her lips, looking into my eyes, but she said nothing.

I shut the laptop and put it on the table. Angry over my failure, I let it clatter to the hard surface instead of setting it down gently. "Let me walk you home. It's late."

Without the laptop serving as a barrier, Addy seemed so much closer. Her thighs pressed into mine as she curled up on the couch, and her breast pressed against my arm. That put her face and those full lips only inches away.

God, why can't I have her?

She had never lost her appeal, even after months of telling myself that she was nothing more than a little sister to me. Deep down, I knew I fed myself bullshit, that she was a mature young woman who had already felt my cock plunge deep inside her. No matter how hard I struggled to pull my thoughts back to an appropriate place, the memory of her pouty lips stretched over my rigid flesh hovered behind it all.

I might even lose my job over this project failure. What does it matter if I sleep with one student? Odds are no one would find out, anyway.

The longer we sat together, silent, staring into each other's eyes, the longer the inner voice in my mind had to convince me that I should let myself experience bliss with her one more time.

She must still want it. I can feel it underneath every word we speak to each other and every look we share.

Addy still hadn't responded to my offer to walk her home, but her lower lip quivered for a moment and she bit it for a second before she whispered, "Landon?"

That uncertain voice was filled with both trepidation and lust, and it awoke the animal inside me.

"You have one chance to take me up on my offer, Princess. Otherwise, you're mine."

That made Addy bite her lip even harder, and her hips shifted as she squirmed in the seat. The movement rubbed her breast on my arm and her eyes fluttered.

"How do you want me, sir?"

Those were the magic words.

I didn't bother issuing her any commands or prolonging the inevitable. I needed her.

With urgent hands, I wrapped my arm around Addy and hauled her into my lap, our mouths crashing together in an electric play of sheer attraction. Two months of pent-up need lashed out as the incredible heat between us dialed up immediately.

Addy swung her leg over my body so she could settle fully into my lap, pressing her lithe body into mine. As my tongue teased her lips, she moaned into my mouth in such a desperate, needy way that my cock hardened in mere moments. She rode on top of me, pressing herself down onto my thickened shaft and panting as she broke off the kiss.

I leaned forward to fasten my mouth onto her neck, licking

and nibbling and teasing her as her hands came to the back of my head and she writhed in my lap.

"Oh, yes, sir. I needed this so badly."

My cock was harder than it had ever been. It had been two and a half months since Addy and I had fucked for the first time, and I'd rejected all other advances since then. It was the longest I'd gone without sex since I was a teenager coming to Harvard for the first time. I couldn't get the girl out of my mind, and somehow, I knew it would all come back to this.

Our need was so great that extended foreplay was nowhere on the radar. Addy's tight yoga pants were in the way, and I gathered the fabric at her inner thighs and pulled as hard as I could until the crotch ripped out of the pants.

"Oh, my God!" Addy stared into my face, shocked, then looked down. "Did you just rip my pants?"

"I'll buy you new ones," I said. My hands never stopped working, pulling her panties aside and running a fingertip up her soaked lips to circle her clit.

Her eyes rolled back into her head and she gasped. "You can do whatever you want, just don't stop touching me."

The sound of her pleasure threatened to pop a vessel in my cock from how hard it had grown. With my free hand, I fumbled with my belt and fly, pulling my member out as quickly as I could. Only then did I remove my fingers from her pussy to replace them with my head at her lips.

I held it outside her entrance, rubbing her clit and enjoying the smoothness of her lips on the sensitive head of my cock.

Addy groaned and shifted her hips, trying to capture me inside her. "Please."

One of my hands slid up her side to wrap around her neck, not enough to cut off her oxygen or blood, but so she could feel it there. "Please, what?"

"Please, sir. Please fill me. Fuck me, take me, use me. I need it, sir. I've waited so long for this."

"Good girl," I said and pressed forward, letting my cock penetrate her.

"Uunf. Fuck!" She gasped so loudly that I worried about Nick hearing her, but I lost focus as her tight pussy slid all the way down on my cock until she was firmly and fully seated in my lap, her ass on my thighs.

"You feel incredible, Princess," I said.

Addy's head had fallen back, and a shudder ran through her body as she convulsed.

"I thought I remembered how big you were," she said, rising up on her knees a few inches before settling back down. "But I can't believe how good you feel."

Words failed us then, communication exchanged with breathy gasps, fingertips digging into shoulders, and soulful looks into each other's eyes. Addy ground down on my cock nice and slowly, taking control as we built each other up.

It was everything I knew it would be, and internally, I struggled both with why I'd waited so long to do this and why I'd let it happen at all. Eventually, I stopped thinking entirely and just let the sensations roll through my body as Addy rode me.

"I need to come, sir," Addy whispered, breaking the verbal stalemate.

She'd been writhing on top of me for an uncountable length of time, the slow build unlike anything I'd felt before. Just knowing she was mine again, that she was asking permission to climax on top of me, was enough to bring me near the edge.

"Do it, Princess," I ordered. "Come for me, and you'll push me over the edge. I want to feel your pussy gripping me."

She shuddered at my words as though I'd broken a dam, and all restraint left her. With a final few hard thrusts on top of my cock, she collapsed forward into my arms, biting my neck as spasms wracked her body.

Her pussy clamped on my shaft like a vise, becoming impossibly tighter and hotter. It was too much to bear, and my own orgasm followed. With tremendous jerks, I shot deep inside her, making her moan and bite me harder.

Labored breathing was the only sound in the house as Addy lay on top of me, spent. Her shirt was still on—we'd never taken it off. In fact, we were both almost fully dressed but covered in sweat from the exertion of mating so intensely.

"Holy fuck," Addy said, finally lifting her head from my shoulder. The skin of my neck throbbed where she'd bitten it— there's no way that wouldn't leave a mark.

"You could say that," I said.

Now that the tension was released, I could think more clearly. My mind was not completely back to normal—my cock was still buried in her pussy, after all—but enough to know that no matter how poor of a decision this may turn out to be, I couldn't regret it.

I'd grown attached to Addy, and this felt right.

"It's late, Addy. Do you want to stay here?"

Eyes wide, Addy nodded.

ADELINE

So cozy.

Pleasant dreams faded quickly beyond conscious recall as I cracked an eye open. There was a heaviness and a stillness that suggested an early hour.

A glaring red digital clock face backed up that feeling.

Three in the morning? Gross.

Then a heavy frame shifting behind me jostled the bed slightly and a warm arm curled around my waist.

I smiled. Landon was a better bedmate than any other guy I'd spent a night with. My eyes drooped closed, but something prevented me from falling back asleep. There was still unfinished business to take care of.

The grant application is due in five hours.

Landon had been so defeated, so despondent about it. He tried to hide it, but after two months in each other's company, I could see past his facade.

There has to be something I can do.

Careful not to wake the slumbering stud, I eased my way out from underneath his arm and fought to find my clothes in the dark. It was a struggle, especially since I'd been so tired while taking them off that I hadn't paid attention to where I'd tossed them.

Only when I put my foot through the crotch of my yoga pants and a faint rip signaled more damage did I remember Landon's barbaric treatment of the expensive clothing.

Shit. I'll totally make him buy me a new pair.

Blinking the sleep out of my eyes, I felt my way through the door and down the stairs. There was enough light coming from the streetlamp through the window that I could make my way to the laptop and the couch. I opened the laptop and the screen's brightness flooded the room and my eyes with the brightness of the sun.

"Oh, fuck," I muttered. "That'll wake you up."

For the next couple of hours, I tinkered with the deep learning model, racing to uncover the problems in time to salvage the grant application. With a spark of inspiration, I combed through the sets of learning data, hunting for something out of place.

There's something wrong here, but I can't figure out what.

"Addy?"

I jumped.

Nick stood at the hallway door, blinking so heavily that his eyes were closed more often than open.

"Jesus, Nick, you scared me!"

With a jolt, I closed my legs and pulled the laptop more firmly into my lap to hide the tear in my pants and the exposed panties underneath. It was bad enough I was still in his house, but that would open a line of questions I didn't want to deal with.

"What are you still doing here? Where's Landon?"

My mind jumped, fighting for an explanation that used enough of the truth to be believable.

"Um, well, we worked late on the data but still couldn't figure it out. Landon gave up on it, and I passed out on the couch because I was too tired to walk back to my dorm. Then I woke up two hours ago and decided to give it another shot."

Nick accepted the explanation without question. He padded to the couch and sat down. "What have you figured out?"

I turned the screen toward him, careful not to move it far enough away to expose my indecency. "There's something wrong with the data we're using to train the model, but I can't find what it is. It's the only explanation, though. You're the software engineer. Do you see anything off?"

Nick's eyes picked through the columns of data, flicking through in half the time it had taken me. Machine learning was his specialty, and he'd helped Landon build the model for his thesis.

"What is this?" He pointed to a row of data.

I stared at it. "I'm not sure. Landon said that was a key component of the inputs, but he didn't get into it."

Nick shook his head and chuckled. "Fuck. All this trouble

over this. Trust me, sis, it's a good thing you didn't go into software engineering. Eighty percent of your time is spent chasing down bugs, and it always turns out to be the stupidest shit possible. This is a row of junk data I put in as an example when I first helped Landon with the model. It's meaningless, but it introduces a random variable that screws with the trends."

I stared at him for a second. "Wait, you mean I can just delete the whole row?"

Still wearing a grin, he nodded. "Back it up first, but yeah, try it."

Frowning, I highlighted the row in the database and deleted it, then set the simulation to run again.

The servers the simulation ran on were powerful, but they were also used by many other projects on campus, so they could take forever to run. This early in the morning, they must have been underutilized, because the simulation finished in only a few seconds.

Scanning the readout, my heart fluttered. Everything checked out. Holding my breath, I set the simulation to run again with the next set of conditions.

Success.

"Well?" Nick asked.

"I can't fucking believe it," I said. "Weeks of bug hunting, and we just had to delete a single row of data?"

He shrugged. "That's programming for you."

The sheer numbers of hours wasted...

"Thank you so much, Nick. I need to get a move on. If I work nonstop, I might salvage this."

He yawned and stretched. "No problem, Addy. I just wish I'd thought to look at this last night. Would have saved you a bunch of frustration."

If you had, then Landon and I might not have gotten together again.

"That's okay, Nick. We can't expect you to solve all of our problems for us."

He stood and strolled to the kitchen. "I'm going to make coffee. I've got to get to the office for a meeting with the team in India. I swear, the next start-up I work for is going to only be based in one time zone."

I barely heard him, setting up the queue of simulations to run on the server. There were only two hours left before the application had to be in. It was already written and just needed the data.

There was still time.

Nick went about his day, getting ready for work and leaving while I feverishly compiled data and adjusted the report to accurately report it. By the time he left the house, I hit send a full fifteen minutes before the deadline.

"I can't believe I got it in." The sense of achievement was uplifting. The project may be Landon's, but I'd spent enough of my time on it to feel like a part of a team. As much as I did it for Landon, I also did it for myself.

Landon.

Exhaustion tugged at my eyelids, sapping my victory and leaving me with no greater desire than to be next to my lover. With Nick out of the house, there was no reason not to.

He was asleep in bed, the sheet barely covering his lower body, the smooth muscles of his torso proclaiming his strength even in their relaxed state.

My heart fluttered.

What would it be like to actually date Landon?

There was no way to tell where this renewed fling would take us. When he woke, Landon could declare it another big mistake and refuse to see me again.

After the first time we'd slept together, I'd known he was special. Upon spending so much time with him and fucking him again, I knew the truth. I couldn't see myself with anyone else—no other man on campus had even come close to touching the pedestal he occupied in my mind.

We can overcome anything together.

I was careful to slip back into bed as slowly as possible, wanting to lie next to him for as long as possible without the possibility of him kicking me out. Once I was in place, Landon shifted, his powerful arm pulling me back against him, enveloping me and cradling me as if I were a precious possession.

More comfortable and cared for than I'd been in a long time, I drifted off to sleep with a smile on my face.

ADELINE

"Now slide your panties off and put them on the desk, Princess."

I stood in the middle of Landon's office, facing away from his desk, where he sat in a tailored suit. After a morning full of sexy emails back and forth, my panties were drenched.

I reached underneath my skirt and hooked my thumbs in my panties, tugging them down my creamy thighs as I bent at the waist so I could look back at Landon.

His eyes were as intense as ever, staring at me as I obeyed his command, roving my flesh so intently that I could almost feel it. A tingle swept through my body as I stepped out of the tiny wisp of lace.

Every day, it felt like I couldn't possibly get more turned on than the one before. And each day, Landon proved that premise wrong. He controlled my body and mind with such ruthless precision that any time he wasn't fucking me, all I could think about was fucking him.

My biggest fear, that he would stop seeing me after we gave in to our urges, had been unfounded. Over the past three weeks, we'd been meeting up every day or two, sometimes multiple times in one day, unable to restrain our lust for one another.

Sneaking around and hiding the affair from everyone around us was the hottest part of it. The thrill of sitting in Landon's class while none of the teaching assistants or other students knew about the carnal knowledge he had of my body was unparalleled by anything else I'd ever done.

Whenever we were in the lab alone together, his pants were unzipped and my skirt was flipped up. Despite the weather cooling down for autumn, I'd continued to wear skirts just to make our trysts quicker and easier to get away with.

His and Nick's house was an ideal place during the day, although the inconsistent hours Nick kept at his company made for some close calls when he came home unexpectedly.

After three weeks, we still couldn't get enough of each other.

I twirled and approached the desk, laying the panties on the middle.

Landon picked them up and felt them. "These are soaked."

Despite not having any real reason to be embarrassed, I flushed. He knew how much he turned me on.

He tapped the desk in front of him. "Sit here, Princess."

I bit my lip and nodded. I loved the way he took control. It highlighted how much power he held over me, and it made me even wetter to please him in any way I could.

"Yes, sir."

I rounded the desk and hopped up on the edge. He remained in the leather office chair before me.

"Lie back."

I did as he asked and gasped as his hands slid up my thighs and spread them open, revealing myself to him. He kissed the inside of my knee tenderly, then gave a soft nibble that sent a bolt of lightning straight up my thigh.

"Mmm, that feels so good."

He continued kissing and stroking the insides of my thighs. I'd grown used to his method of teasing me, but I could never get enough of it. It made the eventual full contact that much more intense, but the wait was almost more than I could bear every time.

After a few minutes spent smothering my smooth legs with attention, Landon drew closer to my lips, and I gasped as he breathed only an inch away from my pussy. I wanted so badly to thrust up and force contact, but I knew from experience that he would only make things more difficult if I subverted his intentions.

This was a game we'd played many times. I tried to hold out for as long as I could as he licked the inner crease of my hip and dug his fingertips into the firm flesh of my ass, but as always, his will was iron.

"Please," I whimpered. "Please lick me, sir."

I could feel the smile in his voice as he licked my hip bone and said, "There you go, Princess."

My hands clutched my skirt, fighting to keep from burying in his hair and forcing his mouth onto me.

"No, not there." My breath came in sharp pants that made it hard to talk. "I need to feel your tongue on my pussy."

No response except for his heavy breath teasing me with an infinitely lighter touch than any finger.

Goddamnit!

The lust had clouded my mind, and I could barely think.

"Please, sir! Please lick my pussy, sir. Please!"

When his tongue pressed against me in a broad, flat stroke, it nearly broke my consciousness from the fiery rush of sensation that coursed through my body in a vicious wave.

"Oooh, yes!" I breathed the words, even in my delirious state aware of our precarious position in his office. "Again, please, sir!"

His tongue returned, and this time, he was relentless. Not in force—he was surprisingly gentle—but in sheer persistence. The masterful strokes and twists of the tip of his tongue painted my passion like a master artist, drawing me further into incoherence until the only thing that mattered in the world was between my thighs.

In what felt like an eternity but also no time at all, my ecstasy had built to incredible heights, threatening to drive me out of my mind with lust. The release followed, plunging me into a world of starburst brilliance unlike anything I'd ever experienced.

The throes of rapture robbed me of the ability to speak or scream or cry out, which was just as well considering the setting. By the time I came out of it enough for my brain to function, my sight was nearly black from the lack of oxygen. A big, gasping breath of air pulled me the rest of the way back into the world.

"Jesus," I said, the word a bare whisper, all I could muster. After a few deep breaths, my voice came back to me. "How the fuck do you do that?"

When I raised my head, it was to meet Landon's as he leaned over me and kissed me deeply. My taste was heavy on his lips, our tongues sliding sensuously across one another as I impressed on him my gratitude for his skill.

He kissed me until I felt recovered and then broke it off. "Are you ready to go on, Princess?"

His voice was still measured but rough. It was a tone I knew well—it conveyed his need. It was my turn to return the favor.

"Yes, sir," I said. After such an explosive climax, I wasn't sure at first if I'd be good for anything else, but his expert mouth on mine had wound me up yet again. He was the most addictive drug in the world, and I could never get enough of him.

"Good. You've interrupted some important work, Princess. Kneel under my desk. I want you to practice your deep throat skills as I finish up a few tasks."

I grinned at the order. It was a fantasy I'd confided to him a few days earlier, to be the teacher's pet, the slut who sat underneath the desk to suck off the professor while he attended to important matters—what goody two-shoes girl *hadn't* fantasized about that at some point or other?

With as much grace as I could muster, I slid to the floor in front of him, kneeling on the ground and backing up underneath the desk until I couldn't cram myself back any further.

He rolled forward in the chair, pressing forward until his bulge was mere inches away from my face. I licked my lips.

Unzipping his pants wasn't enough—his cock was too big to pull out through the hole—so I had to undo his belt and unbutton his suit pants. By this point, I was well-acquainted with his monster secret, but it still awed me every time I hefted it.

Landon wasn't looking down at me, making good on his word to attempt to attend to work while I practiced my skills.

Let's see if he can keep that up.

After a few licks up the outside of his shaft, I opened my mouth as wide as it could go and took the head inside, swirling my tongue as I rotated my hands around the base, giving as much sensation as I could. I enjoyed taking my time when giving him oral, but this time, I wanted it to feel so good that he couldn't do anything but lean back in his chair and look me in the eye as I serviced him.

Wasting no time, I plunged down, fighting past the gag reflex as I'd been practicing until the head of his cock pressed against the back of my throat. With a deep breath, I pressed even harder, pushing until it slid past the tight ring of muscle and into my throat.

A deep groan from above signaled part of my success, but Landon's eyes were still on his monitor. I pushed even harder and took another inch, but there were still a couple left. Ignoring the need for air, I bobbed rapidly up and down, taking it further each time until my lips were almost to the trimmed hair at the base of his shaft.

"Fuck."

It was barely audible, the whisper from above, but I swelled with pride at making him break his stoicism.

Finally, I had to come up and gasp for air. My hands worshipped him as I did, enough cock for one more hand if I'd had another one.

I slid it back down my throat, pushing to get it all the way. When it was at its deepest point, the door to the office opened.

"Excuse me, Professor."

D.G. Whiskey

LANDON

Addy's mouth and throat drove me to such distraction that my eyes were staring past the monitor, unfocused as I concentrated on the unbelievably intense sensations surrounding my cock.

The door opening made me snap to reality, and I watched as a familiar male freshman edged inside. I knew him, but I couldn't place the face. "Excuse me, Professor."

My jaw snapped shut from where it had been hanging.

Addy forgot to lock the door. Fuck, this is bad.

There was no way the student could see her head, otherwise he would have said something by now. Addy hadn't moved since the interruption, her warm mouth still around my cock.

Her panties still lay on my desk, beside the keyboard. Hopefully, it just looked like a random pile of fabric.

A random pile of lacy silk. Totally normal to have on my desk.

"What is it?" I snapped. I would have recognized the boy if

he'd been in my class, so I wasn't inclined to act charitably toward him. He needed to go before he realized what he'd walked in on.

The jumpy way the student responded to my tone of voice triggered my memory, and the next words confirmed my suspicion.

"Sorry, sir. My name's Brody. I'm a friend of Adeline's. We have a group project due tonight that we're supposed to meet to finish up, and I was wondering if you'd seen her. I know she spends a lot of time working on your research."

I cleared my throat. "I'm sure Miss Hudson has found a desk somewhere and is putting her head to work."

A short giggle from Addy vibrated through my cock, and I froze.

Brody's head tilted as if he thought he'd heard something but wasn't sure. I willed him to go away.

After an awkward pause, Brody nodded and backed away. "Thank you, Professor."

As soon as the door closed behind him, I pushed back from the desk, which removed my cock from Addy's mouth.

"Hey!" she said. "I wasn't done with that yet."

"You forgot to lock the door," I said, pointing out the obvious. "That could have ended so much worse, Addy."

She sighed. "Yeah, I know. I'm sorry, Landon. I can't believe I forgot. I was just so wound up by the time I got here that I wasn't thinking of anything else except getting a piece of you."

"I wasn't paying enough attention either," I said. "But I'm still going to have to think of a good way to punish you for this."

With a thoughtful look, she nodded. "Yes, sir."

I stood and strode to the door, locking it once I got there. Then I turned back.

God, she's so fucking sexy.

She remained on her knees, the schoolgirl skirt and tight sweater with plunging neckline straight out of a pornographic fantasy. Her lipstick was a little smeared, and the mascara was smudged from her eyes running while she choked on my cock.

And she was all mine.

"Bend over the desk, Princess," I said. "And spread your legs."

She did as I asked, assuming the position we'd both found we enjoyed the most. There was something so primal about taking her from behind.

I wasted no time—we'd both been spun up enough, and she had afternoon classes to get to.

Her pussy was so wet that I slid in with no problem. In one smooth motion, I was buried to the hilt inside her, pressing against the innermost reaches of her core and splitting her wide open.

I took my time with her, building pace with long strokes, almost completely removing my cock before sliding all the way inside again, the sweet friction drawing us forward. When Addy moaned louder than I liked, I took her panties and gagged her with them. With a hand buried in her hair and another reaching around her body to tease her clit, she thrashed in a powerful orgasm beneath me.

Still, I didn't let up. I fucked her through that climax and into the next, extending her pleasure and giving her no breaks as I built her higher time and time again. After having so much sex in such a short time, my control was endless.

Addy was coming up to a monster orgasm—I could read it in the way her thighs quivered and her muscles tensed and the aggressive way she rocked back into my thrusts. Committing fully to the end, I fucked her as hard as I could, each thrust building my pleasure until I reached the point of no return.

Burying myself inside Addy one final time, my cock exploded within her, and her body was wracked with spasms. Despite the makeshift gag, her moans flooded the room, but I was too turned on to care.

Holy fuck.

Sometimes, the intensity of our fucking surprised me. No other woman had ever taken what I had to give with such determination and satisfaction and given me so much in return. What we had together was special.

As our breathing slowed, Addy peeled her upper body off the desk and let her head hang between her arms. The panties fell from her mouth.

"Oh, my God," she said. "That was insane."

I grunted in agreement, unable to summon more of a response.

We stood like that for another minute as we calmed down.

"Do you have a towel or something?" Addy asked.

"I do, but you're not getting it. And you aren't allowed to take your panties, either. I'm keeping them."

She twisted back to look at me, eyebrows furrowed in a quizzical look. "But you came inside me."

I nodded. "That's your punishment for forgetting to lock the door. We could have gotten caught, so now you must go to your afternoon classes having to worry about me dripping out of you."

She groaned. "That's just going to make me think about this for the rest of the day. And it'll make me way too horny."

"Good."

I pulled her off the desk and turned her head to the side so I could kiss her deeply. Her mouth was hungry, sinking into a deep kiss immediately, tongue against mine. As we kissed, I pulled out of her and let her stand so she could come into my arms. Our kiss ended on a surprisingly tender note.

"Is this ever going to be more than just fucking whenever we get a chance?" Addy's face was unreadable as she looked up at me.

I'd asked myself the same question countless times. What I wanted and what I knew must be were diametrically opposed, and I hadn't found a solution yet.

"We need to be careful, Addy," I said, unable to offer more.

She nodded. "I know."

With an abrupt turn, she strode to the door and unlocked it, letting herself out.

D.G. Whiskey

6
LANDON

The scents floating upstairs were heavenly.

One of the best side benefits of living with Nick was that when the stress of start-up life became too great, he found that cooking was the most relaxing thing he could do. He didn't just toss a couple of things into a pan either. He got downright gourmet with it, finding intense recipes that used fancy ingredients and advanced techniques.

The more involved his brain had to be with the food preparation, the less room he had to worry about work.

Shutting my laptop and rolling out of bed, I skipped downstairs.

"Have a bad day at work?" I called out, rounding the corner into the kitchen. "That smells even better than usual."

I stopped short at the door. The ass in tight jeans bending over in front of the oven did *not* belong to my roommate.

"Hey, man, that hurts," Nick said from the living room.

"There's no way Addy can cook better than I can."

Addy rose with a steaming casserole dish in her mittened hands. "Okay, there, champ. You keep believing that. I've been learning directly from Mom for the past six years. You remember how good her cooking is, right, Landon?"

My stomach rumbled. Their mother's cooking had haunted my memories for years. The meals I'd spent around their kitchen table as a child were countless.

"How could I forget? Your mom was the reason I didn't starve as a kid."

A shadowed look passed over Nick's face. To anyone else, it would have sounded like a harmless joke, but there was a hard truth under the surface.

"I'm almost done," Addy said. She swatted my ass. "Now get out of my kitchen so I can finish dinner."

"All right, all right." I went to join Nick on the couch.

He flipped through the channels until he found the Bruins game. "Seriously, though. You remember how good Mom's Thanksgiving dinners were?"

I hadn't had a proper Thanksgiving dinner in years. Not since the last time I spent the holiday at their house. "I still say she used magic to get her gravy tasting so good. Man, I miss those."

Nick opened his mouth, but I cut him off with a gesture.

"I know what you'll say, Nick. You've invited me back every year, but I'm not going. Besides, plane tickets must be insane this last-minute."

My roommate gave me a wry grin, and Addy leaned in the doorway.

"Tell him, Nick," she said, arms crossed and a broad smile on her angelic face.

Instead of speaking right away, Nick pulled an envelope from underneath the pillow beside him.

"Happy Thanksgiving, Landon. From Addy and me. And my parents."

I took the envelope, feeling pulled into a situation I didn't want and couldn't back out of.

Plane tickets. Return from Boston to Boulder for the long weekend.

"We bought three pairs a month ago but didn't want to tell you too far in advance and give you time to wiggle out of it."

I looked from face to face. "I can't accept this, Nick."

He cocked an eyebrow. "It's already paid for, buddy. Don't tell me you'll let it go to waste and break Mom and Dad's hearts. They're so excited that you're coming back for the holiday."

He had me trapped, and he knew it. I shot a look at Addy to find a similar look of triumph on her face. The familial resemblance was uncanny.

Deep down, I was touched in a way I couldn't show on the surface.

"Thanks, guys. Of course I don't want to disappoint your parents. It'll be good to see them."

Addy twirled, eyes sparkling. "I told you he'd do it! Now go wash your hands, Nick. I know you're a filthy animal."

Nick rolled his eyes and got to his feet. "You really are turning into Mom, you know that?"

"Is there a problem with that? Mom's awesome."

He laughed. "I guess you have a point there."

Once he left the room, I got up from the couch and walked up to Addy. "Addy, I don't know if this is a good idea."

She set her jaw. "We need to spend more time outside your bedroom and your office, Landon. It'll be good for you. Good for both of us."

"Yes, but... What about Nick? And your parents? It's not like we can really be together properly without raising suspicions."

"So? At least we'll be together. That's enough for me. We've had a lot of sex. I want more than that."

She had a point. We didn't have any longer to discuss as Nick returned.

"I'm so fucking excited!" he said. "I've been trying to get you back to Boulder for years. It's a long time coming."

I shrugged. "It's not my favorite place in the world."

Nick put a hand on my shoulder. When he spoke again, his tone was more subdued. "If it gets too overwhelming at any point, just let me know and I'll help you get your mind off it, okay?"

"That won't be a problem," I said, forcing my mouth into a smile. "I'm over it. Let's eat, shall we? It smells delicious, Addy."

ADELINE

This is so amazing. All of my favorite people in the same room.

The only thing that would have been better was if I could tell my parents and brother about the incredible connection that Landon and I shared. Instead, we had to sneak shared looks over the turkey and touch feet under the table.

"It's so good to have you back, Landon. We love seeing you in Boston, but there's something about having all of you kids back in the same house. We were beside ourselves when Nick told us the news." Dad had always been a stern but fair father figure to the boys, providing the structure that Landon had lacked at home.

Landon couldn't have known that my parents talked about him all the time. They were as invested in his future as they were Nick's, and they never failed to ask for updates on their son's roommate.

"It's true," Mom chipped in, passing the stuffing to Landon. "We've always considered you to be part of the family, and it makes us so happy that you and Nick have looked after each other for all this time. And now for Adeline to be in your class! It's like a dream come true. If only you all weren't across the country."

Landon accepted the stuffing and the comments with grace. "Thank you so much, Debbie. It means a lot because I've always looked at you and Jack as role models. I honestly don't know what I would have done growing up without you. If you hadn't let me spend so much of my time here with your family, I would either be dead or in jail."

That stilled the room for a few seconds, but we recovered quickly. "Why don't you tell us about your research, Landon?" Dad asked him. "Adeline mentioned that she's helping you with it. I hope she's not being too big of a pain in the ass."

"Dad!" I felt heat come to my cheeks.

Landon and Nick both laughed.

"She's been wonderful," Landon said. "My research uses machine learning to determine better strategies for corporations. It's still in its initial stages, but it's been very promising so far. Nick donated a lot of programming help to get the idea off the ground for my PhD thesis, and now Addy's pitching in to move the research further along, so it's really a team effort. Actually, if it weren't for Addy, I may have missed a grant that was vital to keeping the project going, so I owe her my job."

That made me blush. "I don't know about that. You would have found other funding. You're basically the poster boy for the economics department. You're just being dramatic."

Landon shook his head. "No, really. You've been incredible. You're more of a partner than an assistant. You've got a bright future ahead of you no matter what you focus on."

"Aww, that's so sweet, Landon," Mom said. "We're so proud of Adeline. But look at you! Not that you were ever not handsome, but you look so put together now. The ladies must be all over you!"

He looked good. With a well-trimmed beard and styled hair, the fat he'd lost since high school gave him a sharper, more chiseled face. He was dressed in a fitted sweater that showed off his broad frame.

Landon shook his head but smiled. "Thank you, Debbie, but it's not like that. I'm just a professor of economics. There isn't anything too special about me."

"Oh, I don't buy that for a second. Adeline, don't you agree that Landon's a catch?"

I did my best to maintain an air of innocence as I spoke with a straight face. "Whoever he's seeing must be the luckiest woman in Boston."

Landon rolled his eyes.

Nick frowned. "You know, I still haven't met this new girlfriend of yours who's been hanging around so much. Somehow, I always just miss her."

After such a short glance in my direction that I could have imagined it, Landon turned to the rest of my family. "I think you'd like her."

Mom wouldn't let it go at that. "Come on, Landon. Tell us more about this mystery woman!"

He smiled. "She's one of the smartest women I've met at Harvard. At the same time, she's so beautiful that sometimes it doesn't seem possible. She turns heads wherever she goes, but somehow, she isn't conceited. She's always stopping to help those who need it, no matter how much it inconveniences her. She's so good that it drives me to be a better man."

I blushed at Landon's first sentence, and by the time he finished, my face could bake the apple pie for dessert.

Luckily, the attention was still on Landon, and I fought to get myself under control.

"Damn, man," Nick said. "Does she have a sister?"

"Sorry, just a brother. And he's a real piece of work." Everyone laughed, but Landon winked at me and we shared special extra laughter at the inside joke.

The rest of dinner passed without incident, but it felt so warm and friendly and *right* that I had to fight not to be overly affectionate toward Landon. Even still, I was worried that my attraction may be noticeable.

Then again, Mom and Dad were used to me fawning all over him when I was younger. It might not be any different than normal.

By the time dessert was packed away, everyone looked just slightly uncomfortable at the amount of food that had passed over the table and into mouths.

Nick, Mom, and Dad settled down at the kitchen table,

pulling out a deck of cards. It was a Thanksgiving tradition—once they sat at the table, there was no getting up for hours.

"Before cards, I think I'll take a bit of a walk," I said.

Mom frowned. "It's cold and snowy out there, Adeline. Someone should go with you. Nick, keep Adeline company."

Nick sighed. "I really don't want to. I just sat down, and this food baby in my belly is weighing me down."

"I'll go," Landon said. "I could stand to walk off dinner, and it would be nice to get fresh air. That was beyond excellent, Debbie. I haven't had a meal that good since the last time I was in this house."

As I expected, the rest of the family showed relief on their faces. Going out into the cold was the opposite of what they wanted after feasting.

"Oh, bless your heart, Landon. Take care of Adeline, and we'll see you back here soon."

After suiting up in warm layers, Landon and I walked into the street. The snowfall had faded to a purely cosmetic level. Flakes drifted lazily to the ground sporadically, but there was a thick layer of snow that crunched under our feet as we turned left and strolled into the quiet.

White puffs of breath froze in the air and floated away, marking the chill as if the white carpet underneath didn't give it away.

Landon looked around, shaking his head as he examined the surroundings as if trying to figure out if it was real or a television set.

"What are you thinking about?" I asked him.

It took a handful of seconds to get an answer. "I spent countless hours running along these streets with Nick growing up, but I never expected to come back."

"You know, I was always disappointed that you never came to visit. Even for the funeral."

His lips sealed into a thin line, but it lasted for only a moment. "There was nothing for me here. But that's changed. I wanted to spend this time with you, Addy."

He stopped and pulled me to him. Our kiss was soft and sweet, so uncommon for us.

"Thank you for the things you said about me earlier," I said, looking up at him. "You are more than I deserve."

He shook his head. "We deserve each other, Addy. That's becoming clearer every day."

After another heartfelt kiss, I grabbed his hand and led him further along.

LANDON

My carnal desire for Addy was everlasting and eternal. That made it hard to think beyond the realm of immediate need and into the future when we were together. At this moment, with the chill and quiet surrounding us and a profound silence between us, it was easier to give thought to where it was all going.

I'd never intended to get so caught up in Addy. One night was all it was supposed to be, and even then, I'd known that was more than I should have allowed. Somehow, I'd deluded myself into thinking it would be temporary even when our torrid affair began and we started sneaking around, stealing every possible moment to be with each other. I insisted that it was just naughty fun, just incredible sex with one of the hottest women I'd ever laid eyes on.

After spending so much time with Addy, I knew now that I could never willingly end things. The troubling thing was that there were so many ways it could go wrong, and a sense of impending doom was inevitable. Even knowing, I couldn't push the brakes, couldn't slow the exhilarating rush toward destruction.

I was so lost in my thoughts and comforted by Addy's hand in mine that the first tombstone to pass us caught me by surprise.

She had steered us into a graveyard.

"Addy, where are we going? If you want privacy to hook up, we can go somewhere a little more suitable."

"Keep it in your pants, Landon. This trip is about doing things together that aren't sex."

Then she slowed to a stop, and I looked around, confused. There were a couple of tombstones beside us, snow piled on the top but the faces clear. A few trees dotted the area, breaking up the somber lines of stones.

A tombstone caught my eye. It had my last name on it. And my father's first name.

"No." The word was barely audible, all I could force out.

There they were. Patrick Fraser and Susan Fraser. Both dates of death were on the same day in April, three years ago.

I'd known they were buried in the city. It made sense it would be in this cemetery. I'd never asked because I'd never intended to visit.

Bitter memories that had been locked in a vault deep in my mind broke free, my mental barriers unprepared for the sudden intrusion of reality. I'd spent every day since leaving Boulder trying to forget about the horrible people buried beneath my feet.

I tried to speak, but a growing lump in my throat strangled

the words before they could form. Addy's arm circled my waist, and I leaned on her for support as my knees weakened.

"I thought you should see it," she said, words soft and eerily deadened in the snowy night. "I'm sorry for not warning you first, but I didn't think you'd come if I told you where we were going."

I fought to clear my throat. "You were right about that."

"You have to confront things eventually, Landon. They get to find peace, and it's not right that you have to carry around that baggage for the rest of your life."

A tear spilled from my eye and trailed down my cheek, hot against the cool skin. With an angry motion, I brushed it away. Addy was right. They had no right to affect me and my life. They didn't deserve a single tear.

"I'm glad you came back to Boulder with me," Addy said. "You need a sense of family in your life. My parents always viewed you as their third child. You were around so much that you may as well have been."

"It was better than being at home," I said, voice trembling. "I have scars in my mind that won't ever go away, Addy. My parents were awful people, and they had no business raising a child. No, they had no business *having* a child. I'd never say they raised me."

She took my hand in hers and brought it to her cheek, then kissed it with soft lips. "Those scars make you who you are, Landon. You learned how important compassion is by living with people who had none. Their mistakes aren't yours to repeat."

I put my hand on her cheek and brought her face to mine for

a kiss.

She deserves the best of everything I have.

I ended the kiss. "I want to make more of an effort to be a real couple, even if we need to hide it from everyone for now."

Addy smiled, a brilliant, heartwarming thing of beauty. "I've wanted nothing more in my entire life."

7
LANDON

Question sixteen. If the supply of money increases, what happens in the money market?

I scratched my chin. Was that too easy of a question for a final exam?

A quiet two-toned chime signaled a new email. That particular notification was the one I used for Addy, and after sending so many sexy messages to each other, simply hearing it engendered a Pavlovian response. Blood coursing to my manhood made it twitch as I changed windows to open my email.

The physical response of my body was vindicated by the image that graced my screen. Out of habit, I looked over my shoulders even though I was alone in my office.

We'd been flirting all morning, as usual, but this was one step further. Addy had sent a picture of herself naked, kneeling on the floor of a spacious bathroom. Her long, brunette hair was artfully tossed over one shoulder, and the seductive pose she'd struck immediately set my mouth to watering. Her pure white teeth bit her reddened bottom lip, a look she knew I died for every time.

"Jesus," I said, eyes darting back and forth to capture every curve in my memory.

The photograph had such an effect on me that it took some time before I noticed the text.

Third floor, east wing. Handicapped bathroom. Waiting for you.

The slight arousal in my pants leapt halfway to full hardness in an instant. With no further thought, I rose and strode to the door, yanking it open so hard that it groaned under the sudden motion.

Turning from the smaller hallway my office was on into the larger hallway running the length of the building, I collided with and nearly knocked down a student.

"Oh, shit! I'm so sorry," I said, putting out a hand to steady him.

When he straightened up, a familiar face greeted me. It was the guy from Addy's classes who was always looking for her.

Not bothering to justify myself, I continued on my way with large, ground-eating strides. Brody faded from my mind immediately, his presence barely a blip in my life as I hurried to get to the woman waiting naked for me.

I took the stairs three at a time, ignoring the looks of students coming down the flights. The handicapped bathroom was close to the stairwell, and within a minute of receiving Addy's email, I was there.

The handle was locked, so I knocked softly on the door.

"Hello?" she said. "Who is it?"

The hall was clear.

"Let me in, Princess."

A click preceded the handle turning and the door swinging inward. I slipped inside.

Addy looked just as she had in the picture. Having her in front of me, seeing the way she looked at me like I was the answer to all of life's problems, sent blood rushing into my cock, filling it past the point of erection and into a level of hardness usually reserved for diamonds.

"I don't have a lot of time, but I needed you, sir," she said, her hands already at my belt.

There was never a moment when I didn't feel the same about her. If all my body needed for sustenance was her taste, then I would never be able to leave.

She had gotten a lot of practice at taking my pants off over the course of the term. My eyes slipped closed as her warm mouth enveloped me.

As good as her blowjobs had been the first time we slept together, they were even better now. Months spent fucking at every opportunity had allowed each of us to learn the other's body to a finely tuned level unmatched by anything I thought was possible.

Addy never acted as though putting my cock in her mouth was a favor or something I was privileged to be allowed. She made love to it, and her faint moans showed just how much she adored pleasing me. From plenty of experience, I knew if I reached down to touch her pussy, it would be completely soaked from how turned on she was.

That enthusiasm sent shivers through my body as I fought down the rising pleasure, wanting to extend the encounter longer to give us both what we wanted.

"Just like that, Princess," I murmured. "Suck my cock. Show it how much you love to take it down your throat."

My words spurred her on, and she choked herself on my shaft as she pushed it down her throat with as much force as she could bear. The additional stimulation was rapidly too much to bear, and I used my hands in her hair to pull her off my cock before she pushed me over the edge.

"It's your turn, Princess."

ADELINE

I stared up at Landon, ravenous.

He did this to me all the time. Just as I sensed my reward for a job well done coming near, he would stop me. I never regretted it because he fucked me so well, but it always took a few seconds to get over the feeling of being robbed of what I had worked so hard to receive.

Landon's hands were still in my hair, and he used his grip to tug upward and force me to my feet. Then he led me to the sink and bent me over it so that my face was in the mirror.

My eyes could barely focus, and my expression was so full of wanton lust I didn't recognize it.

With strong, guiding hands, Landon forced my legs apart, and then he knelt behind me.

"You are so wet that it's dripping down your thighs, Princess."

His words turned me on even more.

"I want you so badly, sir. I can't help it. I need to feel you in my pussy."

He growled and licked my wet thighs, groaning at the taste before attacking my labia. Unlike his usual strategy of teasing me until I begged, he devoured me from the get-go. The intensity with which he licked me, frantic and yet gentle on my sensitive folds, drove my own passions higher. The way he acted like I was an elixir that would stave off death was the hottest thing I'd ever experienced.

Then he did something different. His tongue drifted higher, running up from my clit to my opening in one broad stroke before continuing upward. Before I could register what he was doing, intense pleasure radiated from somewhere I'd never felt it before.

"Oh, my God!" I said, shocked but unable to do anything other than grip the sink harder.

Landon slid a finger inside my pussy as he tongued my ass, his finger the perfect length to press exactly against my g-spot, making my entire body shudder at the combination of sensations. When his thumb brushed against my clit, I convulsed harder.

"Fuck! Yes, sir. Please don't stop."

The triple attack gave me no choice but to grit my teeth and accept the pleasure coursing through my body. It coasted through me in waves, catching me in the throes of a gigantic storm as I did my best to ride it out. In mere moments, I was cast into delirium as Landon coaxed a powerful climax from my body with his skilled fingers and mouth.

He stilled his movements as I came down from my peak, but he didn't give me long to recover. Before I had caught my breath, his cock slid through my folds, the head getting wet from my juices, ready to penetrate me.

We'd had so much sex that I no longer felt any discomfort from the entry of his massive cock, only pure pleasure. He slid into me with a long, smooth stroke and immediately launched into an aggressive attack on my pussy. After such a brilliant orgasm, my body was more than willing and ready to accept his plunging manhood.

Landon grabbed my hair with one of his hands and pulled it back, once more forcing me to look in the mirror as he fucked me. This time, I could also see him standing behind me, his upper body still clad in his shirt and suit jacket, his broad shoulders swaying as he drove himself into me again and again.

His other hand made its presence known when his thumb circled my asshole, teasing the ring of muscle there and pushing gently against it. We'd done nothing like this before, although we'd discussed it. I couldn't believe it felt as good as it did—the moment his thumb popped in, my breath left me in a low, hard moan.

The fullness inside me was unparalleled. Landon dominated my body, and I would let him do anything he wanted. Luckily, the only thing he wanted from me was to give my body more pleasure than I could handle.

With steady strokes, Landon built upon the first climax,

edging me closer and closer to another peak, one push at a time. I fought to keep quiet, aware that anyone could walk by the bathroom door at any time, but it was one of the most difficult things I'd ever done. Eventually, I resorted to turning my head and biting my own shoulder, the pain even lending itself to an intensifying of everything going on.

It didn't last long. The effort to keep from making any noise led to an internalization of the maelstrom within, and my eyes rolled back into my head as I shook. If it weren't for Landon's hand releasing my hair and wrapping around my waist, my knees would have collapsed from the spasms that rocked my body.

The orgasm lasted for at least a full minute, and Landon continued to thrust and work his thumb the entire time, giving me no break but extending my pleasure for so long that it almost felt like I'd entered another phase of reality.

As I came back to earth, Landon sped his hips for a last few thrusts, then pulled out and pushed me to my knees. I'd only just regained enough of a sense of what was going on to position myself and take his cock in my mouth a second before his own climax hit.

Our scents and tastes mingled together as I worked his cock, feeling it jerk in my mouth as his load blasted inside me. By the time it slowed down, my heart rate had fallen from the dangerously high levels it had hit moments before.

"Good girl, Princess," Landon said as he took his cock out of my mouth. "That was hot as fuck."

I looked up at him, happy to have pleased him. "If that's what happens when I send you naughty pictures, then I must do that more often, sir."

He grinned. "I don't think I could find fault in that."

"I can't believe how fast you were up here. It felt like I had just sent it."

"I don't think I have ever moved faster through these halls."

We shared a laugh at that.

Landon straightened up his clothes as I got dressed. He took far less time since he just needed to pull his pants up and redo them, and he watched me with those fiery eyes as I pulled on my lingerie and then my clothes.

"You look like you aren't quite satisfied," I said.

He shook his head. "I'll never get enough of you."

When I finished, he cracked the door and poked his head out. Seeing no one, he walked away without looking back. I grinned as I slipped out and turned in the opposite direction.

LANDON

"Come in," I said in response to the knock.

It was second nature by now. Most professors kept their doors open when they were in their offices, but Addy came by so often that I always left it closed just so that my colleagues were used to it being that way. Getting up every time someone knocked on the door would be tedious.

The door cracked open, and an unfamiliar woman stepped inside. She looked around with interest.

Not a student.

She wore a staff lanyard around her neck, and she was in her mid-thirties.

"Professor Fraser?"

I nodded. "That's right. How may I help you?"

She strode forward and offered her hand. "My name is Margaret, and I'm with the Office for Sexual and Gender-related Dispute Resolution, or ODR for short."

I rose to shake her hand. My stomach felt uncertain at the implications surrounding someone from that office standing where Addy had been naked dozens of times over the term. "Please, call me Landon, and help yourself to a seat. What can I do for you, Margaret?"

I waited until she sat in the offered chair before seating myself behind the desk.

"Well, there's no easy way to say this, but our office has received a formal complaint about sexual misconduct with a student."

The fears that had been hovering in the back of my mind for months solidified into a terrifying reality. "Really? From whom?"

I didn't have to fake surprise.

I've been fucking a student, but there's no way Addy would have made a formal complaint. How did they find out?

"It was made by a third party with very solid evidence."

Is she trying to tell me as slowly as possible?

I shrugged. "I'm sorry, but you'll have to be more straightforward with me. Can you please just lay out the who and the what?"

Margaret had the grace to flush.

"I'm sorry. The student is Adeline Hudson, and the complaint was made by another student, Brody Harrington. He submitted an email chain between you and Miss Hudson as proof, and well…" Margaret got even redder. "Let's just say that it appears to bear out the complainant's claims."

That son of a bitch must have sneaked into my office when I left the other day and ran into him in the hall. I can't believe I didn't lock the screen before I left.

Usually, it would lock itself after only a few minutes of inactivity, so I rarely bothered. That was a costly mistake that I may regret for the rest of my life.

Conflicting impulses tore at me. I wanted to deny the charges and pretend as though Brody was full of shit. At the same time, I wanted to own up to it to protect Addy and then hunt Brody down and rend him limb from limb.

Fighting to maintain calm, I did neither. "What happens now?"

"You will have a week to submit a written response to the complaint. After that, the office will interview you, Miss Hudson, and Mr. Harrington, as well as any witnesses named by you three. After gathering all the information, we will put together a report and issue it to the faculty. The Dean will then make the decision as to what happens next."

"Have you spoken with Adeline?"

Margaret shook her head. "I wanted to touch base with you first. I trust that you will remain professional as this matter is investigated. It goes without saying that until the process is finished and the Dean has made his judgment, you are to cease all personal interaction with Miss Hudson."

I nodded. "It goes without saying."

The veneer of civilized calm on my face hid a firestorm of

emotion. It took all the energy I had to hold it back until Margaret closed the door behind her.

Is this the end of my time at Harvard?

Was all the running around and sex worth it? There were only two things I cared about—my academic career and Addy. Keeping both was impossible, and at this rate, I might not be left with either.

If it came to a choice between the two, which would I take?

8
ADELINE

Boston had somehow so far avoided any of the massive snowstorms that had plagued it in recent years, but that didn't mean that it wasn't cold out. I missed wearing the skirts of the summer and autumn, mainly for the way Landon would take advantage any time I was near him, but there was no way I was freezing my ass cheeks off just to make sex more convenient.

Even with jeans and a coat, I shuffled along the paths between buildings as fast as I could to escape the cold.

"Hey, Adeline!"

The call was from nearby, but it took me a moment to track it down. The hood I'd put on muffled the voice and the direction enough that I didn't know whom to look for, or from where.

By the time a figure bundled up in a big parka with mittens and a hat stopped next to me, I'd almost given up and resuming walking.

"I didn't think you would stop," Brody said. His long hair

was the main thing I used to identify him, and with it tucked under his hat, I hadn't recognized his face.

"What's up, Brody? I already told you I submitted the project, so we're all good." I was shorter than usual with him to hurry the conversation along and get out of the cold.

He waved off my words. "Yeah, I saw the message. I just wanted to let you know that I did you a big favor."

There was something *off* about the look on his face. He was looking at me differently than usual, and it made me uncomfortable.

"What are you talking about?"

"I went into Fraser's office and found your email chain, so I used it to submit a complaint to the faculty. He's a goner, so you don't have to pretend you want him anymore." He wore a big grin now.

As soon as the words penetrated my mind, my hands clenched tight into fists. Dreadful fury filled me, and I forgot all about the cold. I was so enraged that I couldn't even speak.

Brody either didn't see my expression or was as oblivious to its true meaning as he was to every other signal I'd ever given him that I wasn't interested. Instead of turning tail and running like he should have, he forged on.

"I saw your pictures as I read it, and goddamn, you are just as hot naked as I thought you'd be. I might even let you buy me a drink for saving your ass like that."

Conscious decision-making fled me as rage took control.

With a wordless cry, I flung my fist into his grinning face as hard as I could. He fell backward and a spray of red colored the pristine snow beside the walkway.

"How fucking dare you!" I screamed as I jumped on him.

With all the strength in my body, I rained down punches that missed as often as they hit because of the tears that welled in my eyes and obscured my vision. I resorted to clawing at his face with my nails, determined to do as much damage to the arrogant asshole as possible.

The flurry of attacks had caught Brody off balance, but he managed to shove me off him. We both got to our feet and stared at each other.

"You fucking ungrateful bitch!" Brody yelled, clutching his face.

Blood ran between his fingers, and I felt a savage glee at the evidence of damage. It wasn't enough for me. He was trying to assess the extent of the damage, and I took a full windup and a step and rocketed my foot into his crotch.

This time, he went down with a whimper, collapsing in place and twitching, curling up on the ground.

I flung myself toward him again, but before I could inflict any more damage, hands grabbed me and pulled me back. Other people in the surrounding area had responded to the commotion and arrived to break up the fight.

"If I ever see you again, I will fucking cut your balls completely off, you asshole," I screamed.

The looks on the faces of those around me were shocked. I didn't care, shrugging off the arms holding me and sprinting away. A few shouts followed me, but no one gave chase.

Brody hadn't given me many details, but there was only one person I needed to see. I didn't stop running until I reached the Littauer Center. Landon's office was on the second floor, and I choked back tears to regain at least a facade of normalcy for the sake of those I passed in the halls.

Landon's office was locked. I knocked on it, then pounded, but there was no response.

His teaching assistants were located in the same small side hall, and I stuck my head inside.

"Josie, do you know where Landon is?"

The teaching assistant looked up and frowned. "He left in a hurry just a few minutes ago. What's going on? You look like someone died."

I didn't answer, rushing down the hall and back out of the building. He and Nick were only a fifteen-minute walk from campus, which meant I could run there in about five minutes.

By the time I got to the house, I was breathless. Dodging the car in the driveway, I ran up the stairs to the porch and charged into the house.

I found him in the living room on the couch. His eyes widened as I rounded the corner.

"Addy? You shouldn't be here."

"Like fucking hell I'm not. I just beat the shit out of Brody.

Now what will we do about this?"

Landon's jaw dropped.

"You did what? I have to admit I was close to hunting him down myself. I'm glad you took care of him, but it doesn't matter." Landon shook his head and his shoulders slumped. "There's nothing we can do, Addy. They have the emails. The only thing I can do is admit it was all my fault and make sure you don't suffer any consequences for this."

I couldn't believe what I was hearing. He wouldn't fight it?

"It's not like you should take the fall, Landon. I'm the one who started this whole thing, who convinced you to fuck me. I won't let you lose your job over this."

He wouldn't meet my eyes. "It doesn't matter what you say, Addy. The policy's clear on this. I'm older, and I'm part of the faculty. That I'm your professor and also technically your boss makes it that much worse. This is all on me, no matter what you say. They know we've been having sex, and I just have to hope the discipline isn't too bad."

A creak and a heavy step behind me stopped my heated reply short. I whirled to find Nick standing in the hallway wrapped in a blanket, his eyes bloodshot. His face was blank.

"I stayed home sick today, and I overheard everything. What the hell is going on?"

Oh, my God. As upset as I'd been, the possibility and consequences of Nick finding out hadn't even crossed my mind. *I even passed Nick's car on the way up the driveway. How could I be so stupid?*

"Nick." Landon's voice was strangled. "I'm so sorry you had to find out this way, man. Addy is the girl I've been seeing."

I reached out to my brother, but he shrugged my hand off, his attention focused on Landon.

"How the hell could you sleep with Addy after I asked you to help protect her?"

Crossing my arms over my chest, I stepped between them. "Nick, calm down. I'm the one who initiated everything. Landon tried to do the right thing but I wouldn't let him."

"Oh, I'm not holding you blameless either, Addy," Nick said. "Landon has been my best friend since we were two years old. He's like a brother to me, and I thought he was like one to you, too. It makes me sick to think about how you could even bring yourself to do it."

Landon had gotten to his feet, his large presence close behind me. The doorway was getting crowded.

"Come on, Nick, I understand it's hard to take all at once, but it's not that bad."

Nick shook his head violently. "Save it. I'm going to go take some pills to knock myself out, and hopefully, the world will make sense in the morning."

He turned and shuffled back up the stairs, refusing to make eye contact as he went.

My heart had taken a pounding, and there was only one source of comfort nearby. I turned to Landon. All I wanted was for him to hold me and tell me we would work it out, that everything would be okay.

"You should go, Addy. You aren't allowed to be here."

I fought back tears, but they resisted my attempts and spilled over, leaving hot trails on my face. Landon didn't look much better off, but that didn't help the situation. Everything had changed in the course of an hour.

We stared at each other for another half-minute. Reluctantly, I turned to go, walking slowly, ears straining to catch him calling me back.

The words never came.

D.G. Whiskey

LANDON

"Please, Dr. Fraser, sit down."

The Dean of the Faculty of Arts and Sciences, Dr. Koomen, gestured to the plush seat across the desk from his own chair.

"Thank you, sir."

I settled into the seat, apprehensive but less nervous than I'd anticipated. The past few weeks of the investigation had wrung all of that out of me. At this point, I expected to be fired and had resigned myself to that outcome.

"I hope these past weeks haven't been too disruptive to your work," Dr. Koomen said. "I've been keeping an eye on you, Dr. Fraser, and your models have real potential. It's exactly the kind of forward thinking Harvard strives to cultivate."

I blinked. It wasn't the way I expected him to start the conversation.

"Uh, it's been going as well as it can. Dr. Cotton taking over my course for the interim has freed me to put all of my time into the project."

Losing myself in work was the only way I could avoid thinking about the crater in my heart where Addy used to be. It didn't help that every piece of the research had traces of her touch on it, but it was better than sitting at home and getting angry at how things had turned out.

"Good, good. Well, as you know, we've conducted as many interviews as we could and compiled all the data. From the report the ODR issued me, it appears as though you kept this relationship surprisingly under wraps. If it weren't for Mr. Harrington entering your office while you were gone, no one would have had anything more than suspicions."

I couldn't prevent myself from gritting my teeth. "Forgive me if I'm not very happy with his part in all of this."

The Dean's lips twisted in a wry smile. "I suppose I can give you that much. A mitigating factor in this is that judging from the preponderance of evidence—interviews with you and Miss Hudson, as well as the email chain that Mr. Harrington submitted—the relationship was entirely consensual. In fact, judging from Miss Hudson's reaction to hearing the news and the injuries Mr. Harrington sustained, his contention that she was being coerced does not hold water."

That at least brought a smile to my face. The little prick had gotten what he deserved. Addy would get a light wrist slap for assault, but the judge had ruled that she was provoked with the hacking of her personal images and her account of Brody's words.

"However, the relationship did still occur against the rules, and you were Miss Hudson's professor and had also given her a position of research assistant underneath you," Dr. Koomen continued. "In addition, there were many instances of questionable wording in the communication between the two of you that played with the power dynamics of those relationships."

It irked me that over half a dozen people had read the exchanges between me and Addy. It wasn't uncommon to roleplay off the idea that she was performing for marks or a better evaluation, but it wasn't serious.

"As I mentioned in my interview, in no way did that ever affect her marks in the course. She's a good enough student that she needs no extra help."

Dr. Koomen nodded. "And that assertion was backed up by your teaching assistants. Now that we've touched on the salient points, let's move on to my decision."

The nerves I thought I'd swallowed came back in full force. The tone of the conversation had been more genial than I'd anticipated.

Maybe there's some hope after all.

"Whatever discipline you recommend, up to and including my dismissal, I will accept," I said. "I made a grave error, and I apologize for disrespecting the faculty's rules and threatening the integrity of this institution."

"You are perhaps the brightest young star in the economics department," Dr. Koomen said. "I don't want to throw you out over a small issue like this. You're young, and it's not unexpected that you will have feelings for students from time to time. However, you must not act on those feelings, are we clear?"

"Yes, sir."

"Good. Now, you will retain your position provided you accept the following terms. You and Miss Hudson are forbidden from interacting. Passing each other in the halls may occur, but neither of you is to engage with the other in that event. In addition, a camera will be installed in your office to ensure there are no more breaches of conduct with her or any other students. That is all."

My heart shattered. Until now, the sole consolation I'd held onto was that if I were fired, at least I could be with Addy as I looked for another job in Boston. Now, I was forced to choose between the career I loved or the woman I cherished.

Was sacrificing my career worth a relationship with a precocious eighteen-year-old who had so little life experience? We might make it a year before she realizes she wants someone else.

But it's Addy.

We fit together so well, both sexually and mentally. She made me feel more fulfilled than any woman ever had and actively tried to help me move beyond my dark past. Until her, I hadn't felt emotions that intense in my entire life.

I felt overwhelmed. Sitting in front of the Dean, I said the only words I could.

"I accept."

ADELINE

I paced my room. Since my roommate finished exams early, I had it to myself until I went home for the holidays.

Landon still hadn't talked to me. The faculty had informed me of the results of the investigation and the decision reached. Unlike the typical other half of a sexual misconduct case, I hadn't wanted there to be any investigation at all, but that didn't matter.

Frustrated, I called Nick.

"Addy," he said, voice neutral.

We had reconciled over the past couple of weeks. It took a lot of alcohol and explaining, but I finally turned him around on the issue, or at least stopped his anger. His friendship with Landon was too strong to break over a single issue like this, but they were still walking softly around each other.

"Nick, can you please hand the phone to Landon? He won't talk to me at all. I haven't heard from him since the day we found out about the complaint. If he's paranoid about them somehow accessing his phone records, it's your phone anyway."

"Addy, I don't know. He's been pretty depressed. It's impossible to stay mad at him. It's like kicking a starving puppy. I didn't realize that you were so into each other."

"Just give him the damn phone, Nick."

"Fine, Jesus."

The phone rustled in my ear and I waited through a door opening and then knocking. Muffled voices argued back and forth for a while, and then the voice that haunted my dreams spoke.

"Addy, you shouldn't have called."

I shook my head even though he couldn't see. "Their rules can't hold us back, Landon. We just have to be more careful from now on."

"No. It's too risky, Addy, and we should have never gotten involved."

His words struck deep into my heart.

"Are you turning your back on me? On what we have? Did I really mean that little to you?"

There was a long pause as my heart beat hard against my chest. I wished I could see his expression.

"You mean a lot to me, Addy. But you're young, and you don't even know what's really out there. Your school career is just beginning, and you have so many reasons not to tie yourself to me. My academic career will be torpedoed if we get caught even talking to each other one more time."

The shock I felt was unmatched by anything I'd ever

encountered in my life. The past few months had felt like the start of something great, something strong. Something that would last.

I wanted to scream, to accuse him of being selfish, to say that he had taken advantage of me and was bailing out at the first possible opportunity.

Those were the hysterical rantings of another woman, though. I was better than that. I thought Landon was better than that, too.

"Tell me you don't love me," I said. "I need to hear it."

Silence.

We'd never exchanged those words. I hadn't rushed it, even as the feelings had built inside me. The depth of emotion I felt for Landon had shown me that the shallow high school romances I'd dallied in had been mere farces, training wheels until I found something real. I thought there would be time to fully explore what it meant to love and be loved.

"Addy…"

"Say it!" My voice rose. "Say you don't love me!"

"Goodbye, Addy."

The line went dead.

I stared at it, the tears falling again. With as hard of a throw as I could manage, I hurled the phone across the room. It impacted the wall and shattered, bits of glass, plastic, and electronics streaking in every direction.

"Fuck you, Landon," I whispered as I sank onto my bed and rested my head against the wall. "Fuck you."

PART 2

TEN YEARS LATER

9

LANDON

"It's good to have you here, Landon. Woolven Kleist is excited to see what fresh ideas you can bring to the table."

I shook the offered hand. "It's good to be here, Thomas. Thank you again for the opportunity. I'm excited to get to work and bring positive changes to the company's strategy."

Thomas Kelly was an intimidating man. The CEO of one of the largest multinationals in the world wore a navy power suit, and his balding hair was cut short but did not detract from the force of his personality. A longtime company insider, he had maintained strict control over all aspects of operations since his ascension to the top spot four years ago.

He was also now my boss.

"Your office is right next door to mine in the executive suite. Annie will show you later today. As my CFO, I want to be able to get our heads together on short notice when urgent issues come up. Please, sit."

I nodded. It was to be expected.

Thomas's spacious office had more square footage than the house I'd shared with Nick in Boston. It was spartanly but elegantly appointed, every detail finished to perfection, from the overstuffed leather couches in the sitting area to the velvet drapes framing an elevated view of the Statue of Liberty.

The slight shaking case of nerves I'd woken up with had settled a little but still made themselves felt in every deep breath I took.

They probably won't go away for weeks, if not years.

Leaving Harvard had been difficult. Academia was where I had spent my entire career and felt most comfortable, but I was eager to see what kinds of results my methods could achieve in the corporate world. My research had stacked up the rewards and accolades, but the private sector would be the blast furnace that proved it to be solid gold or a cheap imitation that melted away under the heat and pressure. I couldn't wait to prove myself.

The multimillion-dollar pay package hadn't hurt.

Going from the very comfortable but solidly middle-class professor wage to an executive salary was a huge shock, and it still felt surreal, as if my colleagues had pulled off a particularly impressive stunt and would jump out from behind the curtains any moment.

"As we discussed in your interviews, Woolven Kleist has experienced a rocky few years due to the global climate, and the board of directors is eager for a big, bold change to shake up the status quo and reignite our brand and our business," Thomas continued. "That's where you and your computer models come in. If you can deliver, you'll cement your name as one of the greatest economists of all time."

I gave him a wry smile. "No pressure, right?"

Thomas returned my look with a raised eyebrow. "If you wanted no pressure, you should have stayed in school. This is the real world, and you'll swim with sharks on a daily basis. Failure is not an option."

Okay, no joking around with Thomas. Jesus.

"Trust me," I said. "I will do everything necessary to ensure success."

"Good." He gave me a short, curt nod. "I was the CFO before I took over as CEO, and the management structure is mostly the same. It's the only reason I took a risk on someone with so little management experience. I don't expect you to be a faultless manager off the bat. You will make mistakes, but you have talented people underneath you, and they will help you learn. The number one priority is the rollout of your analysis and predictive models."

That reassurance helped to ease my breath. I was confident in my models and the transformative power they could have on the organization. I'd managed small teams before, but those people hadn't had dozens of people working for them.

"That will not be a problem," I said. "Within a month, we will have the framework in place to truly start making a difference."

Thomas gave me another look. "Let me give you a tip for surviving corporate politics, Landon. Whenever you are making promises or delivering good results, you want to use 'I.' If it's bad news, then use 'we.' Take credit for success and spread failure around. Everyone else will be doing it, and you'll handicap yourself if you don't do the same."

The frank advice caught me off guard.

"I'll remember that."

Not for the first time, I wondered what the hell I'd gotten myself into.

"Now," Thomas said. "Let's go to the boardroom. I've had Annie schedule meetings with your direct reports and their teams all day. First up is Financial Planning and Analysis, and then Accounting, Tax and Treasury, Internal Audits, and Mergers and Acquisitions. After you're done with all of them, we'll reconvene and I'll introduce you to the rest of the executive team."

The executive suite, as a whole, was an extension of the tasteful but spacious style exemplified in Thomas Kelly's office. In downtown Manhattan, with its sky-high real estate prices, the broad, open spaces were more impressive than any opulent furnishings or expensive paintings could be.

Annie met us outside Thomas's office. She'd introduced herself as my assistant that morning when she'd met me with the car in front of my apartment and briefed me on the day's schedule, as well as a refresher on corporate policies that I may need to know for my first day. Her efficiency was remarkable. The way she answered each of my questions gave the feeling that she wouldn't easily be caught off guard.

She was also attractive in a buttoned-up, sexy librarian type of way. I couldn't help looking at her tight blouse a few times, and it hadn't gone unnoticed. The first policy she'd briefed me on was the strict no fraternization mandate between managers and any employees in their reporting organization. Chagrined, I kept my eyes fixed to her face from then on.

"The boardroom is through here," Annie said, walking ahead of Thomas and me. "The Financial Planning and Analysis group is already in there waiting for you."

She opened the door for us.

"Thank you, Annie," Thomas said. I echoed his sentiment and squared my shoulders to project confidence as I walked through the doorway.

The boardroom was huge—it could seat fifty people at the table itself, and another seventy or eighty in chairs ringing the outside wall. A massive screen took up an entire wall, and small microphone pucks were embedded every few feet in the perimeter of the table.

Only twenty-five people sat at the table at the moment, a relatively even mix of genders, slanted toward male. Most were dressed in suits.

A woman in a classy work dress stood from near the head of the table and strode forward.

"This is Rose Woods," Thomas said. "She leads the team, and she worked under me while I was CFO, so I can attest to her effectiveness in the role. Rose, this is Landon Fraser, our new CFO."

She had fiery red hair that fell in slight curls to her shoulders, her face showing slight signs of age but professionally made up to minimize the fact.

"Landon, it's great to meet you at last. I'm looking forward to working with you to implement your vision over the coming weeks." Rose held my hand for longer than necessary, and the way she held my eyes was almost uncomfortably intense.

Annie may play by the rules, but I have a feeling Rose will be a handful.

I didn't know if that was a good or a bad thing yet.

"I'm glad you're on board," I said. "Your department will be the one bearing the brunt of the work in rolling out the new models I want us to use, so we must work closely to make that happen. I'm looking forward to meeting your team and getting started."

With a swift look around the table at the aforementioned team members, I froze at a face across the broad expanse.

It can't be.

It had been ten years since I'd seen those eyes in person, but they had haunted my dreams and memories far too often since then.

Addy.

ADELINE

It can't be. How the hell is this happening?

The breath fluttering in my chest threatened to spiral out of control, and only through sheer force of will did I keep from hyperventilating. Luckily, Rick and Sarah were too focused on the conversation between their bosses to notice my near-panicked response to the new CFO.

Never one to pay more attention to office politics than I had to, the hiring of the new CFO hadn't crossed my radar. Technically, the new hire could affect the way the department was run and make life more difficult for me, but there was no use in worrying about the possibility until there was concrete reason to do so. I had bigger things to worry about.

Now, I kicked myself over my stupidity. Any warning would have been better than this.

It felt like I'd been kicked in the chest.

After ten years of avoiding even any mention of the man on

social media and the internet, he stood in front of me. It didn't look like he'd let himself go. If anything, the time had broadened his shoulders even more. His hair was peppered with a touch of gray at the temples, but otherwise, he looked just as I remembered.

That was a problem.

Emotions that had long been buried surged through my mind, a vortex of love, hate, lust, pain, longing, and panic that took away any possibility of rational thought.

I'm over him. It's been forever. It's over.

I repeated the mantra to myself over and over, calming my racing pulse from dangerous levels to merely frenetic.

Then Landon looked along the table and caught my eyes.

Oh, shit.

The rest of the room faded away, and if anyone spoke, I didn't hear it.

His expression was impossible to read. He'd always been inscrutable, but time had only given him even more of an advantage in that regard.

I didn't dare breathe.

Someone beside him said something to draw his attention, and I sucked in a deep gulp of oxygen. More than just my face, my entire body felt flushed.

That wasn't all.

Am I really getting wet right now? Shit.

Landon's smooth voice rolled across the room and through my body, bringing back too many memories of the orders he used to give me and the commands I would obey without hesitation, no matter how dirty.

Then he turned to the table again.

"Hello, team. My name is Landon Fraser, and I'm the new CFO for Woolven Kleist. I'll tell you a little about myself so you can learn where I'm coming from, and I'll be meeting with each of you over the coming two weeks so I can learn about you and what you do. I was a professor of economics at Harvard researching corporate financial theory, specifically, the application of machine deep learning techniques to determine novel strategies.

"You're probably sitting there thinking—hey, that's exactly what our team does. You'd be correct in that, but don't worry, I'm not here to replace your jobs. My research will be implemented as an aid, a tool to help you do your jobs better. I'll be happy to address your concerns at our individual meetings, but if you have any questions, please get in contact with Annie and she will schedule a meeting with me to discuss them."

During a pause, Landon's eyes fell on me once more.

"I'm looking forward to meeting with you. It will be educational."

LANDON

"Thank you for your time, James," I said. "Please send in the next member of the team on your way out."

The intern nodded emphatically without responding, his hand still shaking on the chair as he hauled himself up. Getting him to fully answer questions was like pulling teeth.

Once the door closed, I turned to Annie.

"Is it just me, or was that way more painful than it needed to be?"

She grimaced. "He'll head back to school in a couple more weeks. I have the feeling we won't be hiring him back once he graduates."

I shook my head. "I'll put a personal veto on that right now. Who's next?"

Even though I asked the question, I knew who was next. I'd had the day's schedule memorized once a certain name appeared on it. Annie handed me a summary sheet that I scanned even though I'd memorized the contents last night.

"Adeline Hudson. Graduate from your own alma mater, both in undergrad and with an MBA from Harvard Business School. Been here for four years, and already promoted three times. She's got stellar performance reviews. She's one of our top performers, and upper management has had their eye on her for some time."

None of her accomplishments surprised me. Addy wasn't one to let her opportunities go to waste.

"Thank you, Annie. If you don't mind, could you please make sure the slides are in order for my presentation to the executive team this afternoon?"

My assistant frowned. "You don't want me here?"

"As you mentioned, Adeline graduated from my alma mater, and we've met in the past. I suspect we'll get to talking about mutual acquaintances and it will be boring for you."

"If you're sure…" Annie gathered her notebook and gave me one more look before opening the door and slipping out.

Before the door fully closed, an elegant hand caught it.

Jesus.

That was the only thought I could muster at the sight of Addy. I'd only seen her behind a conference table at the team meeting, but now I could appreciate the sight of her full body. It was as stellar as I remembered.

Maybe more so.

Addy as an eighteen-year-old had been almost criminally sexy. Ten years later, she'd not only retained that sex appeal but refined it. This was a woman who knew how to weaponize her looks and take advantage of the edge it gave her in a world filled with men.

The tight dress she wore wasn't quite inappropriate for the office, but it was enough that it likely earned her envy from her female colleagues.

And way too many looks from the males in the office.

The thought spiked my jealousy, even though I had no claim on her.

"Addy, please sit."

Glad that my voice was strong and didn't shake like I'd feared, I gestured to the seat across from me.

"I'm glad to see you," I said.

Her lips thinned a marginal amount. "Hello, Landon."

Addy's voice couldn't have been more clipped.

I sighed. "You're still mad, aren't you?"

She stared at me, but she didn't answer beyond folding her arms over her chest. Incidentally, that pressed her flesh together even higher above her neckline.

Is that on purpose? Is she trying to send a message with that dress?

If she was, I was having trouble deciphering what it meant. Was it seductive, or was she trying to taunt me with what I couldn't have?

It was difficult enough sitting across the table without the coldness radiating from her. Ten years ago, it had been impossible to imagine anyone more attractive than Addy, but this older version of her was so much hotter that it was hard to believe.

"In case you're wondering, I had no idea you worked here."

Addy's eyebrow rose. The disbelief was so strong that she didn't need to voice it.

"It's true. I told Nick a long time ago that I didn't want to hear anything about you. It just made me sad. Although he pressed me hard to take this job, and I wonder if this is why."

Nick had changed his tune when it came to Addy and me. After the revelation had time to sink in, he kept pestering me to call her up and mend things until I issued a total block on the subject of Addy.

Still no response.

"Tell me about your work, then," I said.

It's a good thing I sent Annie away. She would have had way more questions seeing this than I want to answer.

"I oversee the financial analysts for the entire corporation and report to Rose. It's my responsibility to set their priorities and assign their work, and I also make sure their numbers are accurate. Then I package it up and make recommendations to Rose toward what the overall strategy for the company should be, as well as each individual department."

I frowned. "So you're not involved with the planning side of the team, but you still make strategy recommendations?"

For the first time, a small smile found its way onto her face. "That's right. And if I can brag a little, Rose almost always uses what I say—taking credit for it as if it was her idea."

That jived with what Thomas had said about the corporate environment. I made a mental note to look into it more closely. The CEO had been impressed with Rose and her track record, but what if there was more to the situation than met the eye?

"I'm glad you're leading the analysts," I said. "That will make my job much easier. You already know the models well and are familiar with how they work."

That caused Addy to tilt her head to the side, a gesture I remembered fondly. I fought down the resurgent emotions it dredged up. "That was a long time ago. I would have thought the models changed a lot from those early days."

All through the conversation so far, a feeling rose within me. I missed Addy more than I'd ever let myself admit. Having her here in front of me and listening to her voice again made me more and more certain.

I wanted her back.

She was more mature, and so was I. This time, I knew what was in my grasp and I wouldn't let it slip away again.

"They have, but it's mostly been surface refinements and the introduction of higher-quality data. The underlying code is mostly the same. You helped shape the models into what they are."

I put a bit of extra warmth into my voice.

Addy looked away.

"I was doing my job."

I chuckled. "You were doing a hell of a lot more than that."

A pink flush crept over her cheeks, and she shifted in another signature move—I always knew when she was uncomfortably turned on when she squeezed her knees together like that and adjusted her position on a chair.

Jackpot.

Addy may play at having an icy exterior, but I could melt that shell. I *would* melt that shell. A few pesky rules won't stop me. Not for something this important.

"Are we done?" Addy asked.

I nodded with a small smile. "Thank you for your time, Addy. We'll be seeing a lot more of each other."

"I hope not. It's never a good sign to have to talk to your boss's boss."

With a carefully calculated nonchalant shrug, I rose to my feet to get the door for her. "You're leading the implementation of my new strategic models. If you didn't want to see me, you picked the wrong position."

10
ADELINE

The longer I looked through Landon's models, the more I realized that he'd been telling the truth. My fingerprints were all over it.

It was bittersweet, looking through the lines of code and seeing contributions I'd made. No matter how hard I tried, it was impossible to remember those times without recalling the searing heat of our affair. Most people never experienced the out-of-control passion that had defined my first year at Harvard.

I can't believe the things I would do for him.

No man since Landon had ever dared to order me around like he had. And none had come close to bringing forth the same level of emotion and sensation he could. It was a dirty, shameful secret of mine that every time I touched myself, I thought of the man who had shattered my heart.

That included eight times just in the week since he'd resurfaced into my life.

But I'm totally over him. Right.

A knock at my door made me flinch.

"Addy? How's it going with that model? Come up with a strategy yet?"

Landon slipped into my office, leaving the door cracked behind him.

I'd been daydreaming about the past for so long that my screen had changed to the screensaver. With a scramble, I wiggled the mouse and coughed, knowing it was already too late to appear like I was being productive.

"Just thinking about which analyst I will assign to each aspect of the project," I said. My voice was a little raspy—it always got that way when I thought about Landon for an extended period.

He cocked an eyebrow as if he saw right through my lie.

"What are you doing this weekend?"

I stared at him for a second. Was he really asking me that? After our history and the way I'd been keeping him at arm's distance, he thought he'd just stroll into my office and ask me on a date?

The fucking nerve of him...

"I'm busy," I said flatly. "Plus, I've got a boyfriend, and seeing each other is against corporate policy anyway. I *know* you wouldn't want to violate that. Some of us have moved on, Landon. Sorry if I haven't spent the past ten years pining after my first-year economics professor."

I leaned back in my chair, mentally patting myself on the

shoulder for standing up for myself and not just caving to the man who made my knees weak and my breath scarce. As accomplished as I felt, a huge, hidden part of me wasn't happy. That part wouldn't let me have a moment of satisfaction before picking apart my own words.

It's not like Rich is really your boyfriend. You've been on four dates with him. And you most definitely have spent ten years trying to pretend you wouldn't be happier tracking Landon down and getting him back at any cost.

Landon frowned. "There's a small machine learning conference in San Francisco this weekend that I was thinking of taking key members of the team to. It would be a useful introduction to the topic for a lot of them. It's not mandatory, though, and I know you know your stuff, so if you're busy then you can skip it."

He didn't even address the rest of what I'd said, and my cheeks burned as I absorbed his words.

"Oh. Uh… well, I mean, if it's for work…"

All expenses paid business travel was never something I turned down. There weren't too many opportunities for it at Woolven Kleist unless in senior management, so a paid trip across the country to California wasn't something I wanted to give up for no reason.

"I'll see if I can shuffle my commitments around. I wouldn't want to miss out on a team trip. It's important that I'm there with my people."

It's not like I actually had plans for the weekend. Except for dinner with Rich, but that didn't matter.

Landon shrugged. "It would be best, but it's up to you. Let Annie know before the day's out if you can make it so that she can make the flight and hotel arrangements."

"I'll do that."

Then Landon leaned against the wall and crossed his arms. The position highlighted the breadth of his shoulders, and I had to shift in my seat to stave off the automatic response of my body at the sight.

"So... tell me about this boyfriend."

Crap.

In a panic, I'd thrown out every barrier I could think of. I should have known he wouldn't let it go.

"Well, Rich is a bartender at a cocktail bar midtown. He works late hours and I work during the day, so we don't get to see each other much, but it's good."

More like he was a Tinder match that I had gone on a few mediocre dates with. But Landon didn't have to know that. Not eager to have to make up any more details, I flipped the question back at him.

"What about you, Landon? Who are you dating? Or are you married yet?"

The questions didn't alter his mild expression, but his eyes grew intense. They reached that fiery quality I vividly remembered. It was the look he got when I was about to be completely dominated.

"I don't date much," he said. "Not since a princess set my standards too high for most women to match."

He didn't wait for my reaction before walking away, closing the door behind him with thunderous care. It was a good thing, because I jerked as if shot by the sound of *that* word coming out of his mouth in *that* tone of voice.

LANDON

I shoved the rest of my clothes into the hotel room closet and shut the door with more force than I intended, the door handle vibrating in my hand as the boom echoed through the room.

Easy, Landon. You've got things under control. No need to go overboard.

It wasn't that I was pissed. I was just frustrated.

Sitting next to Addy on the six-and-a-half-hour flight from New York to San Francisco had been both amazing and far too difficult. Telling Annie to book us beside each other so we could discuss work was the easy part. Spending so long in Addy's company had only solidified my desire, the burning need to be with her.

With so much face time, she hadn't been able to play standoffish the entire time. Even after all this time, I knew how to read Addy. She'd loosened up and allowed the talk to progress from polite conversation to the type of witty banter and back and forth that had made me fall for her.

I pushed the boundaries as much as I could with innuendo, dirty jokes, and seemingly innocent questions that had been carefully designed to remind her of times that we'd snuck off to a random public place to do something naughty. Judging by the constant flush on her cheeks, it had worked.

That was encouraging, and my heart felt as full as it had in ten years, but it also led to frustration. All I'd wanted was to put my hand on her thigh, to drag it up the soft flesh and tease her, make her dripping wet for the entire flight. I couldn't rest easily until she panted my name and begged me for release like she had so many times in the past.

With a deep breath, I got out of my own head and looked around the hotel room. A wry smile found my lips.

Addy's instincts had been right. The only reason I wanted this conference getaway was to open the door with her.

If I were successful, this hotel room would be the site where we finally threw out the past and moved into the future together.

As if on cue, an impatient knock at the door jolted me out of my thoughts.

It looks like Addy has similar thoughts.

Could it be that easy?

Eager, I strode to the door and pulled it open, a grin already on my face.

The disappointment couldn't have been greater when Rose stood on the other side of the door.

"Can I come in to discuss an upcoming presentation?" she asked.

I fought to find a reason to decline, but it didn't matter. She blew past me, walking into the room and wandering over to the desk.

"Make yourself at home," I said. Could she detect the sarcasm in my voice?

The Financial Planning and Analysis manager was in a blue dress, different from the power clothing she wore to the office daily. If I were being honest, she took care of herself, and although she was a couple of years older than me, she carried it well.

Rose picked up the TV remote but didn't use it, instead twisting it in her hands as she leaned against the desk.

"What's the problem?" I asked. "As far as I know, nothing's changed from the program we'd already discussed back in New York."

Rose's lips curved into a smile reminiscent of a lion playing with its prey. "Oh, that's not the presentation I was talking about. You know, when Thomas was CFO, I used to give him extra reports all the time. They would cover the *long* and *hard* problems in the room, and we both found them very helpful."

As she emphasized the words, Rose ran her hands up her body, cupping her breasts through her dress.

Oh, shit. This isn't good.

"Thomas always appreciated my presentations, and I'd like

to give you the same access I gave him." This time, Rose sat on the edge of the desk and spread her legs as she spoke, pulling her dress up to reveal a distinct lack of panties underneath. "How do you like the presentation?"

I was at a loss for a few moments. Rose was a direct report and Addy's boss. If I couldn't find a way to stop this diplomatically, she could make life hell for me.

"I'm flattered, Rose. That would go against company policy though. It's only my first week, and I typically make a point not to break the rules so quickly."

She rolled her eyes. "Landon, no one pays attention to those rules. Didn't you hear what I said? Thomas used to take advantage of this, and I'm telling you to do likewise."

Rose hopped off the desk and took long steps that emphasized the roll of her hips as she approached. When she got close, she reached out with her hand and grabbed my cock through my pants.

"I've been watching this bulge since you started, and I need to have it."

That was too far.

I took her wrists in my broad hands and pulled them away forcefully, and Rose gasped, her eyes on mine.

"Yes," she murmured. "Take me however you want."

I pulled her along as I backed up. She came easily at first but then resisted as she saw where I was going.

"I can't in good conscience do anything, Rose. We will

maintain a strictly professional relationship, do you understand?"

I didn't wait for a reply as I opened the door and pushed her through.

The hallway was empty in one direction, but approaching from the other side was Addy. She stopped dead in the middle of the hallway, took one look at me, one at Rose, and back. Then she turned around and walked back the way she came.

Goddamnit!

I couldn't yell after Addy, not with Rose standing there. And the expression on the older woman's face was downright ugly.

"Goodnight, Rose," I said. "I will see you for the first lecture of the conference tomorrow."

Then I shut the door on her face.

ADELINE

My feet pounded the pavement, internal aggression boiling forth as I imagined a face under each step. They alternated between Landon and Rose.

I can't believe I was going to knock on his door last night.

Nothing made me feel more foolish than to finally give in to my desires, only to see Landon ushering my boss out of his room with a guilty look on his face. At least he hadn't seen how late I'd stayed up with tears in my eyes, unable to fall asleep through the emotional turmoil.

And with her? Fuck, Landon, I thought you said you had standards.

Rose was a parasite who fed off everyone around her to fuel her own sense of accomplishment and advance her career. Everyone and everything was a tool to be used with that woman, and Landon had let himself be dragged right in.

He was supposed to be different.

Was I just blind to it after all the time we'd spent together? I'd never had to see how he dealt with other women. Maybe he'd been a sleaze bag all along and it had been hidden from me.

Landon had tried to sit beside me in the lectures and meals throughout the day, but I avoided him like the plague. Unable to help myself, despite my feigned indifference, I watched him and Rose as assiduously as possible, needing to confirm my suspicions to feel entirely justified in my hate and disappointment.

There had been nothing obvious except for Rose being extra flirty toward Landon. He was a far better actor than she was.

After the final afternoon session, I'd needed something to distract me and help me work through the emotions roiling under my skin, and the run was helping. By the time I got back to the hotel and into the shower, the towering pile of hatred had faded to a dull resentment.

How dare he come after me like he wants me while he's sleeping with my boss?

It was still early for dinner, and I was exhausted from the lack of sleep. The bed was comfortable enough and my body so desperate for sleep that I was out before I even pulled the cover over myself.

Blackness overcame me, a dreamless state that ended only with a loud ringing that flooded the hotel room.

It took a few swipes at the bedside table before I successfully grabbed the phone and accepted the call. Working for a major corporation, it was second nature to answer phone calls any time of day or night. Accessibility was always impressive to managers.

"Hello?"

"I know that voice. I woke you up from a nap, didn't I? Were you a little tuckered out from the sessions today?" Landon's voice was teasing.

My thoughts were scrambled, pulling themselves together out of the oblivion of sleep.

"Um, maybe. What's going on?"

"You're late for dinner. The entire team's out. You'd better get your ass over here."

My stomach flipped. "What? Really? Shit, okay, I'll throw some clothes on and be there. Where are you?"

"I'll text you the location. It's a short Uber away. Just ask for the Woolven Kleist reservation at the front and you'll find us."

Only halfway through getting dressed did I remember that I was supposed to be angry with Landon. The nap had put some distance between it and me, and the immediacy had faded.

I hurried through only the most cursory makeup application and thanked past me for laying out a dress for dinner. It took only five minutes from waking up to calling an Uber.

The restaurant was a swanky place. Fine art and modern wooden and glass dividers split the space into intimate alcoves, and attentive waiters and waitresses were everywhere.

Nothing like dining out on the company dime.

I would never have dared expensing a dinner at a place like this, but if Landon was the ranking manager, it was his expense account bearing the damage.

The hostess led me to the back of the restaurant, then gestured to a single small table set for two.

"Are you sure this is the Woolven Kleist reservation?" I asked. "There's supposed to be ten people here."

The girl nodded. "This is your reservation, ma'am."

"Okay." Not wanting to make the girl wait, I sat down.

As soon as she was out of sight, I pulled out my phone and called Greg, an analyst in my group.

"Hey, Adeline."

"Greg. Where is everyone?"

"Terry and I are having a couple of drinks at the hotel bar. Not sure exactly where everyone else is right now. We saw you rush out a while ago, but you didn't hear us call after you. What are you up to?"

Movement in the corner of my eye caught my attention.

Landon strode toward me. He was a vision, dressed in a fitted pinstripe suit and carrying a few long-stemmed roses.

"Nevermind," I muttered into the phone and hung up. I stood and frowned at Landon. "What the hell are you doing?"

He pressed the flowers toward me, and I took them automatically.

"Please, Addy, sit down."

"I—"

He cut me off. "Quiet, Princess. It's my turn to speak."

That name, again.

Somehow, it had lost none of its potency over the years. It made me want to obey him, to serve him. It turned me on like a switch had been flipped.

It wasn't fair.

Fair or not, I sank back down to the seat.

Landon sat across from me. "I've never been the same since we had to stop seeing each other ten years ago. No matter how I lied to myself, no matter how I tried to convince myself that the hole in my heart was temporary, that it was getting better, I knew deep inside it was all bullshit. When I saw you at Woolven Kleist, it became clear. I've been a fool this entire time. I never should have put anything ahead of you, Addy."

The raw emotion in his voice broke my heart, and I fought back the tears that filled my eyes. The final remnants of the layer of ice I'd cast around my heart to protect it from him melted away—there was nothing I could do about it in the face of his relentless warmth.

"But you did," I said. "You put your career in front of me, and you would do it again. It's more important to you than I could ever be."

If I let myself be drawn back in by Landon, it was only a matter of time before the relationship imploded just like it did the last time.

Landon shook his head. "I'm different, and you're different, Addy. I couldn't be sure back then that what we had would last. I was just starting my career, and you were only eighteen, for fuck's sake. I know you weren't a typical teenager, but if I'd blown my entire life up for you and then you changed your mind, that would be more my fault than yours."

His words made sense, and I'd had those thoughts myself, but it didn't change the way he'd refused to talk to me at all. It didn't change what I saw the night before.

"If I'm so important to you, then why did you have Rose in your room last night?" I asked. "I won't be led around like an ignorant child, Landon."

I surged to my feet. If I didn't run away from this now, it would become impossible. No matter how much uncertainty and anger I held toward Landon, he could sway me like no one else could.

Cutting off his rebuttal, I threw the roses back into his face and fled, finding my way through the maze of a restaurant. It was difficult to navigate through the tears, but I made it out to the street before Landon caught up.

His hand on my arm was rough as he pulled me to a stop and forced me to turn around to look at him.

"I didn't do anything with Rose," he said, his voice intense. "She forced her way into my room, and you saw as I was pushing her back out, Addy. How could I ever even think about being with her when my entire soul yearns for you?"

I looked away, unsure what to think, thoughts tumbling through my mind in a chaotic swirl. The only constant was the anchor of his deep voice. I wanted to be persuaded. Why couldn't I allow him to do it?

"Addy, it's impossible to resist you, but if you walk away from me one more time, I will let you go. I'm not a monster who can't take no, but I won't sit around and be kept on the hook forever. It's now or never. What's it going to be?"

There it was. An ultimatum. Landon had put the ball in my court, and it was entirely up to me what I wanted.

If I turned away from him, would I spend the rest of my life regretting it? Was it worth maintaining my indignation over his choosing his career instead of chancing the whims of an eighteen-year-old girl?

Was there any reason to continue to deprive us of what we needed?

I looked Landon in his eyes. They were full of fire, and his hand still on my arm was hot. I thought about what that hand could do to my body when his eyes looked like that. It crumbled the last of my stubborn resolve.

"Please, sir," I said. "Take me."

He growled as he pulled me to him and crushed my lips with his in a glorious, passionate kiss.

11
LANDON

The journey back to the hotel room had been lost in a haze of passion and the bare semblance of restraint. I hadn't seen any of our team members on the way, but if they'd seen the way we looked and touched each other, there was no hope of explaining it away as anything other than what it was.

When we stumbled through the hotel room door, it was on.

I kicked it closed and wrapped my arms as far around Addy as they would go as our lips found each other and we crashed into the wall. I pinned her there, hands exploring her body, rediscovering the territory as I hungrily devoured her.

The throaty moans she offered as I took what I needed from her drove me crazy, reawakening hundreds of memories that overlaid reality. When I buried my hand in her hair and tilted her head to the side so I could latch onto her neck with my open mouth, she gasped loudly and clutched at my shoulders.

Pressing my thigh in between her legs, I moved lower,

flirting with her upper chest as I gave her something to grind against.

Addy's hands weren't idle, slipping inside my jacket and forcing it off my shoulders, then working the buttons of my shirt, stripping me from the waist up so that she could run her fingertips against my abs and dig her nails into the exposed flesh of my shoulders as I grasped her ass and pulled her body against mine.

"God, yes, Landon," Addy breathed in my ear as our bodies pressed together. Her hands found my hardened cock through my pants. "I needed this so badly, sir."

"You'll get everything you've been waiting for, Princess," I replied. With deft hands, I unzipped her dress and tugged it down her incredible curves. "Over and over again."

She wore simple black panties and a bra underneath, but on her, it could have been thousand-dollar lingerie. The bra lasted less than a second under my questing fingers, and then I knelt in front of her as I pulled her panties to her ankles.

I kissed her thigh right next to her exposed lips.

"As beautiful as I remember," I said, keeping my voice low and seductive. "I've been dying to taste you again ever since I saw you in that meeting room on my first day."

Addy's hands fell to my head, running through my hair as I teased her flesh and licked up her inner thighs.

"What a coincidence," she said. "I've been dreaming about your tongue for ten years."

I growled and lifted her right leg to wrap it around my

shoulder, leaving her standing on one leg while leaning back against the wall as I knelt before her. The position opened her up for me, and she looked too delicious to resist any longer.

"Fuck, sir," Addy moaned as I split her lips with my tongue and took a lazy lick up through the center. "That feels incredible."

I took my time, swirling my tongue through her folds as I kissed, exploring her and reacquainting myself with her likes and needs. Every time she gasped, I noted the location and motion, cataloging and charting the exact methods it took to drive her crazy.

If I'd wanted to, I could have brought her to a shuddering climax within the first two minutes of licking her, but I took my time. Instead of a headlong crash, I built Addy's pleasures and tensions up slowly, varying the pressure and speed of the stimulation to send rolling waves of sensation through her body. The fingers in my hair grasped and squeezed as she guided my head, her eyes closed to focus on the way I played with her pussy.

Eventually, Addy rode on the edge, so close to teetering over and into ecstasy that her hips bucked against my tongue and she forced my head into her harder, desperate for the extra shred of pressure she needed to lose herself.

I obliged and ended the teasing, sucking gently on her clit as my tongue caressed it. Addy shuddered and cried out, her leg around my back tightening to pull my body closer, slight tremors in her thigh showing how close she was to losing her balance.

Tightening my arm around her waist to keep her upright, I

continued my assault, and Addy's cries turned silent as the height of her climax rolled through her. Shudders wracked her body, and her full weight fell on my shoulders as her left leg buckled.

"Jesus Christ!" Addy's breath returned in big, trembling gasps. "I haven't come that hard in…"

I looked up at her and grinned. "Ten years?"

She closed her eyes and nodded with a small smile. "Something like that."

While she recovered from the swell of sensation, I ran my hands along her legs and torso, unable to stop myself from extending contact with her as much as I could. She felt as good under my hands as I remembered, her skin soft but firm, her curves as delectably perfect as ever.

When her breathing returned to normal, she looked at me with an expression I could only describe as ravenous.

"It's my turn," Addy said. "That cock has spent far too long outside my mouth, and that changes now."

Unwrapping her legs from around me, she helped me to my feet and then gave me a hard push. Stumbling backward, I fell onto the bed.

"This," she said, undoing my belt, "is mine now. If anyone else touches this without my permission, we'll have problems, is that clear?"

Eighteen-year-old Addy had been as submissive as anyone I'd ever slept with, but this adult Addy wasn't afraid to go after exactly what she wanted. The role reversal was hotter than I expected.

"Crystal clear," I said.

"Good."

With rough motions, she pulled off my pants and then my boxer briefs to expose my large erection to the open air.

"That's what I've been dying to see. And taste. And feel inside me."

Addy crawled onto the bed, her shoulders and hips swaying from side to side in a perfect pantomime of a prowling cougar.

"It's all yours, Princess."

She didn't need me to tell her so. Addy bent her head to my body and nuzzled around my thighs, kissing and licking and taking her time before getting to the shaft that rose above my stomach waiting for her.

The sensation of her lips and tongue on me was good—too good. It was too early in the blowjob for technique to have any perceptible impact on the pleasure received, and yet the simple fact that it was *Addy* between my legs made it better than any I'd gotten in ten years.

Technique quickly became more important as Addy lined up my cock and sank onto it, forcing her head down until the head of my cock pressed against the back of her throat. Then, she pushed even harder and the impossible tightness of her throat surrounded my cock as her lips sank to the base of my shaft and her nose pressed into my groin.

"Fuck, Princess," I said, letting my hands play with her hair as she swallowed me whole. "You've gotten even better than you used to be."

In response, she bounced up and down a few times, squeezing my head and forcing my eyes to close to deal with the pleasure flooding up my body from the things she was doing to me.

After the initial rush, Addy slowed her style, taking her time to play with my cock. It made it even hotter that she was obviously enjoying it and not just putting it in her mouth to please me.

Five minutes later, I was anxious for more. There was something I hadn't felt in ten years, and the time for waiting was over.

ADELINE

Landon sat up, and before I could even take my mouth off his cock, he had flipped me onto my back.

When he positioned himself over top of me, his familiar weight settled on my body and I let one hand grip his shoulder as the other ran beside his face and pulled his head down to mine.

I could still taste my pussy on his lips, and it turned me on as it always did. We needed no more words between us. As we kissed, Landon's cock slid between my legs, and I spread wide and hooked my heels around his body to welcome him home.

The moment of penetration felt better than I imagined it could. Nothing Landon's size had been anywhere near my pussy for ten years, and it stretched me to the breaking point as I struggled to adjust.

"Whoa," I said. "One second."

He paused, holding himself above me, content with kissing my neck as the searing pleasure burned my nerves, bordering on painful with its intensity.

With a deep breath, I forced my muscles to relax. Landon moved his hips in small, gentle strokes that helped me get used to him. Before long, the strokes lengthened, and I wordlessly encouraged him on with my hands and legs, pulling him deeper into my body as we reforged the bond that had been broken for far too long.

"Right there," I whispered, eyes fluttering and rolling back as his cock pressed deeper inside than I remembered.

This was why I'd done anything and everything for Landon. No one else could come close to the way he fit inside me so deeply and just right, rocking against the most sensitive parts of me and stimulating my body to new heights.

My breath caught in my chest as pleasure consumed me, reducing me to wordless moans as I luxuriated in Landon's conquest of my body.

When we kissed, his expert lips stole my breath away almost as much as his movement inside me. It was overwhelming, sending me adrift in a sea of sensation.

The first time I came, it stole over me almost by surprise, sudden spasms squeezing his cock inside me, intensifying every stroke and feeling better than it had any right to.

The second time, Landon had sped the pace of his hips, slamming into mine with such intensity that I was caught in an endless wordless cry as his skill robbed my voice of its strength.

The third time, I clutched Landon's back and kissed his

neck, begging him to come with me. When my words pushed him over the edge and his cock pulsed inside me, the sheer intimacy and shared pleasure left me nearly in tears at the level of bliss around me.

LANDON

I checked my phone and grinned. Addy's latest message told me how she planned to tease me once we got back to my apartment.

Learning from the last time we'd dated against the rules, in the weeks since San Francisco, Addy and I used an encrypted messaging service on our phones and jealously guarded the passwords. So far, it was working. The spark set off by the conference had ignited dry tinder, and we couldn't keep our hands off each other outside of work.

Inside, we relied on technology to tease and titillate each other. No more office trysts, as hot as they were. We were older and more careful.

It helped that we had our own apartments, so there was no stopping us from spending all of our time outside work together with no one being the wiser.

Careful, I texted Abby. *You'd better behave, or else Princess will choke on cock again for the third dinner in a row.*

She was quick with her reply. *Sounds like a reward to me.*

A knock at the door ruined the mood. My office was nearly as spacious as Thomas's, and the walk to the door allowed my erection time to subside.

"Ah, Rose. Please, come in."

She smirked and walked inside. The woman had remained relentless, ambushing me at every opportunity. It was driving me crazy, and not in a good way. The worst part was that I constantly had a large bulge from the teasing with Addy, and her boss always noticed.

As soon as the door closed, Rose grabbed my arm and pressed herself against me. She rose on her toes to kiss me, but I turned my face to the side and dodged it before firmly pushing her away.

"Rose. What the fuck are you trying to do? Do you really think that's why I called you in here?"

She shrugged, unrepentant. "You'll come around eventually."

I sighed. Dealing with the woman was the one part of the job I didn't enjoy. The rest of it was a challenge, but it was an interesting one that I was growing more and more comfortable with very day.

"Please take a seat, Rose."

She grinned and sat in front of my desk and looked up at me as if expecting some sort of kinky role-play.

That threw me off because of the sheer number of times

Addy and I had role played this exact type of scenario. Somehow, the mere thought of doing it with Rose was repulsive, and it wasn't because she's not attractive.

I sat at my desk. "Since I've assumed the CFO position, I've been taking a hard look at all the numbers coming out of your group. Many of them made little sense, so I've dug deeper."

Rose's grin faded. "What are you talking about?"

"Your reports make no sense, Rose. I know Thomas never looks at the actual numbers, so it's no wonder he never caught it, but it looks like you haphazardly pull random numbers from your team's reports and throw them together. Then you take whatever strategy recommendation Adeline has made and paste it across the top."

All hint of playfulness left Rose, and she took on the look of an animal backed into a corner. "Are you seriously taking the word of one of my direct reports over mine? Adeline is a glory hound desperate to climb the ranks despite not having what it takes. She'll say anything to keep her status as the next big thing."

It took some effort to keep the irony out of my voice. "It sounds like you're projecting your own insecurities onto other people. In any case, I haven't talked to Adeline about this at all. I've come to this conclusion myself after reading all the reports in your section going back several years."

"Bullshit," Rose spat. "She's wanted my job ever since she came to my group. Just because she's younger than me, you're taking her side over mine."

I shook my head. It was almost sad how she clutched at any excuse rather than own up to her actions. "I'm afraid I have to let you go, Rose."

She stood, pushing back from the desk so violently that the chair tipped over and crashed to the floor behind her.

"Just because you have a hard-on for that stupid little slut doesn't mean that you can get rid of me! You do not understand how this company works, and I'm going to Thomas. I will sink you, Landon, and you will fucking remember the day you messed with me. You could have enjoyed some action on the side, and now you'll go back to your pointless life in a lecture hall, not making a lick of difference in the real world."

I stood but maintained my hold on my temper. Rose's hypocrisy knew no bounds.

"Thomas is in Asia visiting the offices there for a week, so you'll just have to wait. In the meantime, you can pack your shit up and get the fuck out of my building."

She turned and stormed out, trying to slam the door behind her but foiled by the soft-close mechanism in the hinge.

I was glad to see her go, but a shred of worry remained. Rose may be a hypocrite, but she was disturbingly close to the mark when it came to Addy and me. We tried to keep things under wraps in the office, but maybe we hadn't been careful enough.

At least there's no chance she has any proof.

12
ADELINE

Life was great.

With Rose's departure, Landon had named me acting manager until a replacement was found. In private, he'd confided that I was, by far, the best internal candidate, and thanks to Woolven Kleist's internal advancement strategy, I was a lock unless Human Resources came up with the absolute perfect external candidate.

The move got me one step closer to the CFO position and the CEO job beyond. Landon, rather than be worried at my ambitions, encouraged them.

"You work harder than almost everyone I've known, and you've got a natural knack for strategy that is rarer than you could imagine. I had to design a set of computer models to help shape strategy, but you have an eye for it that makes you nearly unstoppable," he'd said. "Once you have more experience under your belt, you'd make a better CFO than I do."

His praise of my work ethic and intelligence swelled my heart more than anything else he could have said. Most men only stop to compliment women on their looks, but those are fragile and fleeting comparisons that will fade. Landon never failed to make me feel sexy, but he knew to value me as more than my looks.

That was one reason I was falling even harder for him than before.

Unlike the first time we'd launched into a fast-paced and all-consuming affair, this was more than just sex. We went out for dates in the park and along the waterfront, sampling new and interesting restaurants, and seeing shows on Broadway. When we wanted to stay in, we would watch a movie and cook dinner together in Landon's spacious Manhattan apartment.

I'd spent every night there since we returned from San Francisco, and it was glorious.

And as soon as this meeting is over, we get the entire weekend together.

Greg was wrapping up his report, and I shook off my thoughts as I took back control of the meeting.

"Thank you, Greg. I'll have Terry look into those numbers first thing on Monday morning, and we'll decide if we have to take action immediately or can afford to sit on things for another week. Now, unless anyone has anything else, we are done." I waited for only a moment. "Okay, have a great weekend, everybody."

My bag was already packed, and it took only a moment to grab it on my way past my desk. The weekend mass exodus was in full swing, and several other people stood around the elevator as I walked up.

When it opened on its way down from the executive suite on the top floor, Landon was the sole occupant.

"Landon," I nodded as I entered.

"Adeline."

That was the extent of acknowledgment as people crowded in. I was pressed against Landon at the back of the elevator.

His hand found my lower back and quickly ran down my skirt to play with my ass through the thin material, fingers stroking and softly grasping.

I fought to keep any sign off my face and didn't even dare to look back at him. Thankfully, the others in the elevator kept up a high enough level of banter that my quickened breath drew no notice.

Once the doors opened on the main floor, we walked out into the lobby and took separate directions from the main doors without looking at each other. I walked two blocks west before turning north and followed that until I could loop back east to Landon's building.

By the time I got to his apartment door, Landon opened it for me and handed me a glass of red wine.

"Happy weekend," he said, wrapping an arm around me as he kissed me so hard that I forgot about the wine. It nearly fell from nerveless fingers before I regained my senses.

"Mmm," I said. "If that's a preview of what's to come, it's

going to be a very happy weekend."

He winked. "That's nothing. Why don't you relax while I toss some food together?"

I followed him to the kitchen and sat at the broad kitchen island as he pulled food from the fridge. He'd ditched the suit jacket and rolled up his sleeves. The muscles in his forearm rippled as he wielded the knife, chopping the onions with surety.

Landon's cooking skills in college had left a lot to be desired, but he'd drastically improved since then, and it was crazy how fun cooking with him could be.

The wine was disappearing quickly, and I spoke my mind without thinking about the words coming out of my mouth.

"Fuck, you're sexy when you cook," I said. "I love you."

I froze, unable to believe what I just said.

Landon looked up so quickly that he lost his grip on the chef's knife.

"Shit!"

He jumped backward, his feet escaping harm's way as he scrambled to get out of the way. One of the best skills to have in the kitchen is to train away the impulse to grab at a fallen knife. That was a recipe for a bad cut or worse.

Landon looked up, stricken. We stared at each other for a few seconds before bursting into laughter. Landon doubled over, holding his stomach as deep, booming laughs rolled from him.

Seeing him laugh was enough to keep me going, and we fed off each other for far longer than any normal person would have deemed necessary.

When Landon recovered enough to walk, he rounded the island, still chuckling and smiling. I readily allowed him to pull me into his arms, and he kissed my forehead as he pulled me tight.

"I love you too, Addy."

Then he kissed my lips, and the world fell away as love and happiness enveloped me. I lost track of everything around me, completed by the man with his arms around me.

Eventually, the loud sizzling broke my love-struck daze.

"Hey." I smacked Landon on the shoulder. "You have food to attend to, mister."

"There's definitely something here I want to eat," he said with a wink. "But I guess there's cooking to do, too."

He refilled my wine, and I sipped it again as he worked the pans and continued prepping ingredients.

I can't believe we finally said it.

The L-word had been hovering over us for a long time. Even back in college, I'd thought it, but we didn't get there before we were torn apart.

It was a monumental moment, but it seemed so commonplace. Of course we loved each other. We wouldn't be doing what we were doing if we didn't.

That didn't make it any less special. But it also didn't make things perfect.

"I wish we didn't have to sneak around," I said, swirling the wine in the glass. The deep red liquid spun in a miniature whirlpool before settling.

Landon looked up from his task. "I know what you mean. It's hard to say when that can change, though. If we worked at different companies, we'd be able to date openly, but we would be able to see each other so much less. At least this way, if a problem comes up at work and we're stuck late working on it, we can do that together."

I sighed. "I know. I can't think of a better way. It's just how it has to be for now, I guess."

In the back of my mind, the gears worked, dreaming of how much better life could be.

Landon set a plate of beautifully arrayed beef and vegetables over a savory rice pilaf in front of me, topped up my wine, and kissed me.

Then again, I already have it pretty good.

LANDON

"Landon, come in here, please."

"Yes, sir," I said.

That didn't take long.

Thomas had only been back from his Asian trip for half an hour. It wasn't necessarily a bad thing that he was calling for me to come over to his office so soon, but I couldn't shake a vague sense of worry.

I gave a cursory knock on the door before swinging it open.

"Thomas. How was Shanghai?"

I crossed the room and sat in front of his desk. He ignored my question, reading something on his computer screen. Once I was seated, he looked at me.

"Why exactly did you find it necessary to fire one of the company's best managers and replace her with an unproven girl barely out of college? And why did you do this behind my back, while I was across the globe?"

Shit.

I'd expected a couple of questions from Thomas about firing Rose, but she was my employee and it was my place to fire her. That it was the first thing he brought up after spending a week in Asia was a very bad sign.

"I know you were a big fan of her, Thomas, but Rose had demonstrated none of the skills you'd lauded. She was proven incompetent and unprepared in several big meetings with other departments that I had to smooth over. Looking into her report history, it became clear that she almost always messed up when collecting results from the teams under her direction. As for Adeline, she has received nothing but glowing reviews every year, and she's already been heavily promoted and is on a special inside track for advancement. The strategy recommendations Rose has been taking credit for all year long have been lifted directly from Adeline's reports."

Thomas sucked on his upper lip, then shook his head. "I'm not buying that. It's ludicrous, Landon."

"I can show you all the reports. It's an obvious trail of deceit."

The CEO leaned back in his chair. "I'm not interested, Landon. If it's not a show of blatant favoritism, then how do you explain this?"

He hit a key on his keyboard, and then voices came out of his speakers.

My stomach flipped as I recognized Addy's voice as it

gasped.

"God, yes, Landon, I needed this so badly, sir."

My own voice responded to her in the clip.

That's from San Francisco. How the hell did he get that?

"How could you possibly have that?"

It didn't take long to figure it out. Rose had been in my room, and she'd grabbed a couple of things off my desk before putting them back.

She actually bugged my room?

"Rose," I said, thinking out loud. "She must have planted something when she tried to seduce me so she could blackmail me over it later. This worked out even better for her. She can take us both out with one shot."

Thomas bristled. "Seduce you? I highly doubt Rose would stoop to that."

I fought back my automatic reaction to his wishful thinking, but then stopped.

It's probably all over now. I may as well speak my mind about this.

"Grow up, Thomas. Just because Rose has sucked your dick doesn't mean she would never pull the same trick to get ahead with other bosses. And giving an incompetent employee like her more and more responsibility just because she puts out is the worst management I've ever seen. It's no wonder the company has gone to shit since you took over as CEO."

"How dare you," Thomas said, standing up from his chair.

"Get the fuck out, and kiss your stock options goodbye. Take that whore of a Harvard bitch with you."

My hand itched with the desire to punch Thomas in the face, but that's exactly what the man wanted. He'd sue me faster than I could spit if I assaulted him. Instead, I attacked something much more important to him than his face.

I looked Thomas in the eye. "You will fail. And there will be no one else to blame but yourself. The whole world will know how incompetent you are."

With a smug smile I put on just to annoy him, I strolled out of his office as casually as if we'd just shared a discussion about our weekends.

ADELINE

Numbness had been the overriding feeling ever since security told me to pack up my desk. A quick call to Landon had confirmed it— we'd been caught out by Rose, and Thomas had fired both of us. He invited me to his place to figure out what to do next.

When I got there, boxes in hand, the door was unlocked.

I wandered inside, feeling like a ghost adrift in the world. The past four years of my life had been poured into Woolven Kleist, playing the corporate game and rolling with the politics, putting in long hours to impress people and get ahead, and it was all gone.

Landon must be in a similar state.

All I wanted was to cuddle up with him on the couch and commiserate over how unfair it was. The world just wanted to punish us for being together.

At least he wasn't given a choice between me and his career.

As soon as the thought appeared, I felt guilty for it. Our

relationship was much stronger this time around, and I'd already forgiven him for the chain of events that drove us apart ten years ago. It was done, and there was no changing it at this point. We just had to make the most of the time we had remaining.

Landon wasn't on the couch, but I felt too sapped to call out, and instead, I wandered through his massive apartment.

I found him in the seldom-used dining room, bent over the table, pieces of paper scattered around him. His hand was a blur as he scribbled on a notepad.

Approaching from behind, I scuffed my steps so he would hear me coming and not be shocked when I spoke, but he didn't look up or turn around. I looked over his shoulder.

"Hudson Fraser?"

Landon nodded but didn't look up, his hand continuing its frenetic pace.

I'd seen language like this before. It looked like a company charter.

"Landon? What's this?"

He finished his current sentence with a flourish and sat back. "I've been working on the biggest problem we have—that we can't . be together without worrying what bosses think."

I sat beside him and rested my elbows on the table, cradling my head in my hands.

"Even though we've been fired from Woolven Kleist, that doesn't mean we'll be able to find a job where the bosses are okay with us dating. I'm sure they're out there, but it'll be hard."

"What if we don't have a boss?"

The depression generated from the sudden change in life situation had thickened my brain with fogginess that affected my ability to piece together information, but the playful glimmer in Landon's eyes helped to shake it off.

"Do you mean what I think you mean?"

Landon took my hand. "I'm sick and tired of trying to fit you into my life, Addy."

Pain flared at his words, but he didn't linger on the thought long enough for it to blossom.

"I want to fit the rest of my life around you. The only thing I know for sure is that I want to be with you, to cherish you, to hold you, and to make you feel as incredible as I can, as frequently as I can."

Landon slipped out of his chair and knelt in front of me, edging closer so he could pull me in for a quick kiss. "We work fantastically together, and we need no one else. Will you start a consulting company with me? It won't be easy, and I know we're more technical than sales people, but I think—"

"Yes!" I cut him off. "Yes. I love it, Landon. It's the perfect solution. I would love to start a business with you."

When he'd first gotten on his knees, I thought…

No matter. This is huge.

"I haven't asked you the big question yet, though," Landon said. "Will you marry me, Adeline Hudson?"

My poor heart had been tugged in every direction possible

that day. In one sentence, Landon made it whole again and filled it with joy.

"Oh, my God," I said. I leaned forward to kiss him again, hard. "Yes, Landon. I want to more than anything in the world."

EPILOGUE
ADELINE

"I'm glad you're pleased with the results of our latest strategic adjustment, Mark," I said. "We'll have even more to give you soon."

The youthful billionaire sat in a boardroom a quarter of the way around the world, surrounded by his top executives. The telepresence system projected his image inside our cozy boardroom and sent ours to theirs.

"Thank you, Adeline," Mark said. "This partnership is bearing fruit even sooner than I anticipated, and I'm eager to see what strides we can make from here."

Landon took my hand as he leaned forward. "The reception in the Mediterranean could be better, but if you have any concerns or ideas at any time, please let us know, Mark. And of course, you have a standing invitation to visit the boat any time you need a break."

"I'll let Priscilla know. We just might take you up on that

offer. Enjoy the weather over there."

The connection cut out.

Landon pulled me close and brought me in for a slow, soulful kiss. "You were magnificent, as usual."

I smiled. He was always effusive with his praise, but it was hard to fault him for it. "As were you, my darling."

As we exited the boardroom and walked toward the bow, we passed Maria.

"Ah, Maria. I believe we'll take dinner in the al fresco dining room tonight."

"Yes, Mrs. Fraser." The stewardess bowed and hurried away to make the arrangements.

Landon took my hand and pulled me to the forward sundeck, standing at the railing overlooking the shining sea.

I stood in front of him and settled back against his chest as his arms wrapped around me.

"Did you hear about Woolven Kleist?"

"You mean Thomas getting fired? I'm only surprised it took so long. They've posted losses for two years straight."

I nodded, letting the vindication settle as I enjoyed Landon's embrace and watched the sun dip toward the horizon.

"Is this where you envisioned us four years into our business?" I asked. "Conducting meetings from the boardroom of our yacht as we sail the world?"

Too cozy to look back, I could hear the grin in his voice as he replied, "I just wanted to keep a roof over our heads. I never got so far as to think that roof would be attached to a big yacht. I couldn't be happier about it. I hope you feel the same."

I bit my lip. Was this the opening I'd been looking for?

"Couldn't be happier? Not even a little bit?"

He squeezed me tighter. "Hard to imagine. I'm pretty damn happy right now."

I smiled and turned in his arms to look up at him. "What about a couple of pounds happier?"

Landon held me at arm's length. "What are you getting at, Princess?"

With a concerted effort to fight through the reaction that word provoked in me, I continued, "What if instead of just *sir*, you had another three-letter word I could call you? Like dad?"

"What?" Landon's hands dropped to my belly. "For real?"

"Yes," I said, laughing. "For real."

His arms pulled me close, squeezing so hard that my back cracked. "You're pregnant? You're pregnant!"

The bruising kiss he lay on me left no doubts as to his thoughts on the matter.

I still thought I'd better check. "Happier now?"

With one more kiss, he hugged me tightly again.

"Happiest possible."

ABOUT THE AUTHOR

D.G. Whiskey is a world-traveling writer from Toronto in his late twenties who is happiest when exploring new countries and meeting new people.

Enraptured by fictional worlds since reading Lord of the Rings at age seven, and spurred on by dozens of bookcases packed with his mother's fantasy and romance novels, D.G. has been writing stories for twenty years. With a background in engineering and a passion for writing, he's a firm believer that you should never let yourself be put into a box—you can accomplish anything!

Made in the USA
Columbia, SC
20 September 2019